Confessions of a Pagan Nun

confessions of a pagan nun

A NOVEL

BY

kate horsley

Shambhala
Boston & London
2002

SHAMBHALA PUBLICATIONS, INC.
Horticultural Hall
300 Massachusetts Avenue
Boston, Massachusetts 02115
www.shambhala.com

9 8 7 6 5 4 3 2

Printed in the United States of America

♾ This edition is printed on acid-free paper that meets
the American National Standards Institute Z39.48 Standard.
Distributed in the United States by Random House, Inc.,
and in Canada by Random House of Canada Ltd

The Library of congress catalogs the hardcover edition of this book
as follows:
Horsley, Kate, 1952–
Confessions of a pagan nun/Kate Horsley.—1st. ed.
p.   cm.
Includes bibliographical references.
ISBN 1-57062-719-3 (hardcover)
ISBN 1-57062-913-7 (paper)
1. Ireland—History—To 1172—Fiction. 2. Druids and Druidism—
Fiction. 3. Woman—Ireland—Fiction. 4. Women, Celtic—Fiction.
5. Nuns—Fiction. I. Title.
PS3558.O6976 C66 2001
813'.54—dc21
2001020066

For Aaron

THANKS TO Mark Stewart for consultation on Gaelic terms and Celtic wisdom and to Michael Reed for initial editing; Barbara Daniels for a place to write; Ivan Melada for meaningful encouragement; scholars dead and alive; my teachers Jitsudo Sensei and Aaron Parker Lockwood; Father Roland Teske, SJ, for Latin translation assistance and Biblical acumen; Victoria Shoemaker, my beautiful agent; Sister Mary Minehan of Kildare and her sisters for keeping the flame; Carmel Hester of the Kildare Town Library; Joel Segel, dauntless editor; and Larry Hamberlin for being a stickler. And thanks to those of you who read to children.

TRANSLATOR'S NOTE

OF THE LETTERS and other documents written in the earliest days of Christianity, few survive whose authenticity is unquestionable. Most of these were written in Latin. I give as an example two documents from the same general period as that of the manuscript presented here: the *Confessio* of Saint Patrick, written around AD 450; and the letters of the nun Egeria, who wrote an account of her pilgrimage to the East early in the fifth century for the benefit of her sisters in northern Spain or southern France. Gwynneve, the author of the text translated here, in addition to writing around fifty years after the time when Patrick and Egeria were writing, was near them in other aspects as well: like Patrick, she wrote in and about Ireland; like Egeria, she was a woman whose name and identity are not clarified in any history of her time.

However, the differences are more significant than the similarities. Unlike Patrick or Egeria, who both wrote in ecclesiastical Latin (albeit in different styles), Gwynneve wrote in Gaelic, her native tongue. She was also literate in Latin and Greek, as can be seen in her accounts of her duties. One may speculate that the use of Gaelic, a language so personal and beloved to her, led her to give details of her life unusual in other texts of this time. Whereas there are ecclesiastical narratives that include details of the writer's history (such as those of Patrick and Augustine of Hippo), most of these do so in the service of the writer's conversion to Christianity, as accounts of the author's sin or salvation. Gwynneve's style was clearly influenced by these Christian writers and by Roman documents, such as the detailed and secular writings of those philosophers whom Christian scholars transcribed, but her tone was greatly shaped by the Gaelic tendency toward poetic imagery and emotional revelation.

In this period, the church was nearing success in eliminating the many heretical movements that abounded in the early days of Christianity, including the Pelagian heresy, to which Gwynneve alludes, and the Gnostic heresies, such as the Montanists' movement. The church threatened heretics with severe punishments, including death; that is very likely the reason why this document was hidden and only recently recovered.

The manuscript was found in an excavation near Kildare, in the county of Kildare in Ireland, about two kilometers from the convent dedicated to Saint Brigit. (Saint Brigit was a Christian manifestation of the pagan goddess Brigit and a woman said to have been raised by a druid and converted by Patrick.) The original manuscript is in codex form, a number of parchment folios sewn together and bound in pigskin. Slightly damaged by water stains, it was discovered in a sealed box made of clay and iron, among artifacts in a well or narrow pit used to hold human remains, agricultural offerings, and other religious items. According to local folklore and archaeological evidence, the well had once been the site of a ritual that entailed throwing fresh hemlock into its depths twice yearly, followed by a feast in honor of an unnamed spirit or saint who supposedly gave comfort to the dying and to mothers who grieved for dead children.

The codex, the only one found at the site, has been dated at around AD 500. As stated above, the original is written in Gaelic with a few Latin phrases. Where there is no equivalent word in English, the Gaelic term is retained. A footnote explains the term at its first appearance in the text; a glossary at the end of the book may also prove useful. The Latin phrases have been kept to maintain the original writer's desire to interject them as exceptions to the Gaelic; again, footnotes provide translations. For purposes of clarity and flow, I have added contemporary punctuation, which was not in use at the time the manuscript was written. I have also made a modern distinction between upper- and lowercase letters.

K.H.

Confessions of a Pagan Nun

DECLARATION

I, GWYNNEVE, a sinner quite uncultivated and the least of all the faithful and utterly despicable to many, appeal to Saint Brigit or the goddess Brigit, whatever it is her wish to be called. I pray that she, being the guardian of poets, will bless me with honest and strong words.

I am what is called a *cele dé** near the age of barrenness, when a woman's womb becomes useless and hairs sprout on the chin. I reside in one of a cluster of hives made of stone at Brigit's church, a place of plain beauty but always cold and damp except in summer, when the wind is green. It is a constant temptation for me to pause in my work and stand outside on the hill to see the valley and the waves of hills beyond.

I live and work most days and nights in my *clochan*† with one waxen candle to light the parchment. I labor like an insect beneath its mud dome transcribing scripture, since I am one of a few nuns who are literate. I am fast at my work, for my teacher, Giannon the Druid, was an expert at the magic

---

*Cele dé: a servant of a god, or nun.
†*Clochan*: a beehive-shaped cell made of stone.

of words and taught me both thoroughness and impatience. I have just now completed a transcription of *sciathlúireach*.* There are only a few more hours before the bell will ring for lauds at dawn, but I do not want to sleep. I do not sleep deeply or long some nights, but linger in a netherworld between thought and bestial images. The dead will sometimes speak to me. An agitation overtakes me. At these times it soothes me to write. The relentless thoughts about what I have witnessed and heard find some peace when I turn them into marks on parchment. I cannot keep silent about some occurrences and observations, nor in fact would it be proper to do so. It is a holy duty to know the truth and tell it.

The truth has a volume much larger than one person's body and soul. I am small both in body and soul but will try to be like the ant who carries many times its own weight. Those who read these pages, have mercy on me. *Beati immaculati in via.*†

> The cross of Saint Brigit be under my feet.
> The mantle of Mary be about my shoulders.
> The protection of Michael over me, taking my hand.
> In my heart, the peace of the Son of Grace.
> In my soul, the protection of all good spirits in this
>   fierce and beautiful land.

Sciathlúireach: protective prayers from one of the books of Saint Patrick.

†"Blessed are those of blameless way."

My *túath** was Tarbfhlaith, where I was born to my mother, Murrynn, and my father, Clebd. I can say little of their ancestors, they having been mostly unrenowned in battle, except for my mother's father and his sister. Some have heard of them as Connacht and Flaev. He was a *finna*† to the High King Loeguire, the chieftain who refused baptism when Patrick offered it. Connacht and his sister Flaev were two of the lean warriors who died during the five hungry years. My aunt, it is said, stood before her brother to protect him and was cut in the legs and fell. Connacht, revealed behind her, received an ax blow to the mouth, which severed his head at the jaw. Flaev lived for several days while the cruel hatred of her enemies, which had entered her through the wound in her leg, reached her heart and smothered it. The heroic deeds of Connacht and Flaev were woven into the songs our men sang at feasts while they beat the table with their fists.

I loved the look of the men's fists and the roar of their

Túath: tribe made up of one or more kinship groups or clans.
†*Finna*: royal bodyguard.

voices. I loved how the women at these feasts tore their robes and revealed their breasts in celebration of sacrifice and lust. For many years, I perched on my elbows beneath the feast table to hear the names of my grandfather and my aunt sung. But the lines of the songs were repeated so often that they became as common as straw. After traveling to other places, I learned how small my *túath* was. The chieftain's hall, in fact, was no more than a hut longer than the scores of huts that seemed to have tumbled into a mud clearing beside the lake called Oille. I could not be so loyal and devoted a member of the *túath* of Tarbfhlaith as others, who were content to sing one song their whole lives and speak often of pigs and oats. Since I was a child, I have wandered far from my *túath* and even became *fortúatha.**
I still have a place in my eyes for the strong oak and pine that embraced my *túath* and a place in my nose for the smell of the soft grass beside the furrowed fields. But my attachment to the people of Tarbfhlaith flowed from me slowly and steadily like water from a cracked vessel. Many feasts became contests between those who drank too much ale and accused their neighbors of pig killing or stealing, for our meat and bread were precious and not sure to sustain our lives, though a man or woman worked from pink light to gray light to provide one meal. Few were like my mother, who raised her face up from her food bowl to look at the stars or hear the lark go deeper and deeper into the forest.

My mother's influence never leaves me. I cannot now

*Fortúatha: of the alien people.

hold her warm hand, so I will tell of her character. In all the writings I have transcribed, there is no account of such a woman. I do not call her a saint or a hero, but a good mother who died at the beginning of the great changes, leaving me with an unredeemable loneliness. Let me honor her here in case there be no other place where she is honored, for she did not die with her head severed at the jaw, nor atop a large horse, nor in any manner likely to be lauded in chieftains' halls or Christian manuscript.

I confess here that my mother was not Christian, but in her time there were few who knew of the replacement of our gods with the three gods in one. She worshiped not God but what He created, and she knew plants well but not as a scholar. The tonsured men were not yet here to give the plants their Latin names. My mother knew them by their true names: *fraechoga, crem,* and *birer.** When there was sickness in the *túath,* many were glad to see my mother's slender feet walk the mud paths between huts with her bundles of herbs. As a small child with limbs that seemed too thin to be of any use, I went with her into the forest while my older sister tended the pigs. My mother taught me to smell the earth she held in her hand and understand the odor of fertility, to compare it with the odor of barrenness. She showed me the brown, infertile circle in the forest where small creatures who live mostly under the ground pour out their spite in dark rituals of purification. She said to me more than once, "A soul cannot live with too much

_____

Fraechoga, crem, and *birer:* woodberries, wild garlic, and watercress.

spite in it, just as a body cannot live on food that is too bitter." The sometimes bitter creatures who caused painful mischief for us were the ancient ones who had grown small and were led by their queen, Bebo. There were still eruptions of the timeless and fierce fights between Bebo's subjects and the great ones who also lived beneath the earth with our dead heroes. They still argued over stolen cattle, so long dead that even their calves' calves were turned to dust, though these stories are still told at feasts and even translated by the Christians, who concede their power over the people of this land. But my mother spoke of the ways of gathering pleasure from a hard life, not of ways of stealing livestock. She was not ashamed of her beauty or to rub her hands with perfumed oil or to leave a feast when men's war tales went on too long.

Even as a child, as light as straw and hardly expected to live to womanhood, I had no interest in the stories of raids upon various kingdoms for the purpose of owning one bull or another. I occupied myself instead with the mystery of places and beings we cannot see as we see a tree or a horse or a cup or a man. I could ask my sister or my father about the health of the pigs, but I went instead to my mother and asked if the forest were endless, if the stars were the eyes of creatures in the sky. I asked if my grandfather were sitting at a banquet table beneath the ground with his head severed at the jaw. Terror curdled the milk in my stomach when I thought about him unable to eat the fine food served there, meats and cheeses at every supper. Since then I have dreamed of my grandfather and my aunt sitting with Our

Lord Jesus Christ at the Last Supper. In this dream he is enraged that his jaw will not close and allow him to eat, and so he turns the table and spills all the food onto the floor. My mother did not claim to know the condition of her father in the afterlife, nor what the dead suffered or did not suffer. She shook her head sadly when she could not give an answer, and she took my hand in hers and pressed it as though to shape it. She said once, "Stop your thoughts! Watch the clouds drift into different forms." And I did so, giving her time to dig the roots that she used to put flavor in our food bowls. She was a clever mother who could give both to herself and her child at the same time.

When a white flower emerged and stood bravely between the muddy indentations made by hogs' hooves in the pens, my mother said, "Here is a message for you, Gwynn, that not all beauty is trampled before it can show itself among the pigs."

When we passed a dark pool, she could tell me which spirit lived there, perhaps the spirit of an ancient one who regretted the loss of its human form and sought to grab a child to inhabit. There were also spirits who listened to wishes and tried to fulfill them by saying certain words in their dark waters. The words came up as bubbles to the surface. As I followed my mother to these places, I kept my eye on her black hair draping her shoulders and back like a fine cloak hiding a tattered robe. I was afraid of losing her in the deep woods, for, as I said, I was small and frail; but she treated me as though I were strong, striding forward with no concern that I would fall behind or be snatched by a more sturdy entity than myself. It was my mother's assumption that I was not weak that made my bones solid and encased my spirit. Once she told me, "You are very clever, Gwynn." She told me this as though it were a wonderful and dangerous secret. She warned me to use my cleverness to be free from the obligations of a woman married to a man who raises pigs, or at least to keep secrets from him. For she had a life apart from her husband, my father, though he knew little of it except for the praise of those whom she made well with her herbs. Sadness gathered in her face when she looked at me long, as though she could see events that she could not prevent from wounding me.

In those days no one else looked into my eyes or endowed me with strength. The other members of my household believed in terror as a method of binding us together, telling stories of horrible deaths, of the loneliness of corpses, of the pain of disease and of the cruelty of the elements: winds that ripped a man's arm from him, famines that caused a woman to eat her own child. To point to the world's punishing suffering was to give a necessary lesson. To point to a person's weakness was to inspire him to be strong. So my father and my sister told me that I lived too much in dreams and that my breasts would never be large enough to please a man or nourish a child. My father accused my mother of starving me by filling me up with stories instead of food. Everyone in my *túath* was hungry, especially during the months of thick frost. But I did not want food as much as I craved her stories, which soothed me. I listened to my mother weave words together and create worlds, as though she were a goddess. Words came from her mouth and dispelled my loneliness, even when she was not with me. She began every story with the phrase, "It was given to me that . . ." When I asked her who had given her these stories, she rattled her *cíorbolg*,* in which she kept small oiled stones that she claimed entertained her with tales. I began then to know words as immortal things one could see and touch, each having a color and shape like a pebble that never suffers disease or death. I dreamed of bags of polished pebbles; each bag a story; each bag holding one precious jewel among the many pebbles or a dark, black stone that was death's eye.

My father and sister and others in the *túath* tried to teach me that I loved words too much, but what I loved was the freedom of words. Even the man who stole a brooch from the chieftain's daughter and was put in a cage made of pine branches had words, the curses that he flung at children who squatted in front of him to learn about the appearance of thieves. Even a man in a cage can speak words, or if his tongue be cut out, hear them, or if his ears be filled with dirt, have them in his mind. In words he is free at least until he dies, and I do not know, nor did my mother, if a man has words after he is dead, other than what he has left behind in his writing, if he were literate.

I see no reason to live other than to be free. A person does not have to do anything in this life but die. He may defy everything but death. If death proves that I am not free,

---

Cíorbolg: comb bag for women.

[9]

then I praise Our Lord Jesus Christ for overcoming it, though I still do not know where my grandfather might be and with what difficulty he eats his eternal feast. I still wonder where the dead who drew my love to them like a golden thread from my belly have gone, why they are so silent. I still feel them pull my organs. I look for them beneath the surface of pools in the deep woods and would happily give them my body to inhabit, for sometimes I would rather be bound by death than by loneliness, and sometimes I wonder if death itself is not the greatest freedom.

In the last years of my mother's life, she was on our region's council of women and therefore traveled once a year to the Fair of Tailltenn. In those days there were a women's council and a men's council at which their *túaths'* concerns and secrets were discussed. I went with her only twice before worms diseased her. In those years I was too young to attend the council and waited for her beneath the tree of the druids. The first year my mother began to train me to be a member of the council. When we walked the road home and stayed the night in the public hostel situated on the crossroads where the eastern road crosses the northern road, she made me look into her eyes. She reminded me that our eyes were poured from the same pool, colored deep like green holly. She told me of the words that the women say at the start of their meetings and the order in which the women may speak. There were long portions of our walk home on the northern road when she said nothing, not even giving up a story. Her eyes and nose and mouth seemed to drift closer together in a solemn concentration. A laugh would leap from her like a bird flying suddenly from a branch. The branch moved but was empty, and I felt then that I would starve if my mother did not feed me with her words.

In the second year that my mother took me to the Fair of Tailltenn, she had become wild with weariness and a resolution to live at least some of her life without any fetters. When she was away from my father, who tethered her with his fears, she went feral, like a wolf who has been domesticated only in its fur but not in its flesh. She even howled once, tossing her hair back and lifting her face to a moonless sky as I stared at her and shivered. At the public hostel she met with men in ribald activities such as drinking mead provided by the *tánaise*.* She laughed well at the satires told by the druids, old satires about dead men with no heirs, which were not dangerous to hear. She held me close when we went to a corner to sleep and whispered in my ear that people needed herbs and stories and sometimes ale to overcome their pain. I could see the pain beginning to take the place of her stories and desire for knowledge.

I learned soon that no one, not even the most beloved of a chieftain, is free from worms, treacherous falls, vicious animals, or sorrow.

The freest humans I observed were the *aes dána*,† who attended the Fair of Tailltenn and could travel from *túath* to *túath* without fear of being attacked or turned away. They

---

Tánaise: next in line to be chieftain or kin.
†*Aes dána:* druids and their companions.

were not caged by any loyalty. They transcended political and marital affiliations and saw the severing of a warrior's head at the jaw not as tribal glory but as part of an eternal mystery much larger than one *túath*'s reputation. Druids were able, it was said, to stop warfare with a black fog and transform a man from king to fool with their satires, words so powerful that they cut more deeply than swords.

The poems and stories of the druids went far back to before the time of anyone's grandfather. They knew histories and geographies, rituals and prophecies so great as to make one man's mortal life seem like a small feather dropped by a bird who is sleeping with its head tucked inside its wing. The druid's power was knowledge, and the druid's knowledge came in words. I began then to lust for the druids' power. For if one does not have knowledge of what to do or think, he will be told by another what to do or think. It is my greatest challenge to obey what another tells me, may God forgive me. My mother's fingers holding herbs, stained by the black earth she dug them from, and her merry mouth, one side curling up, are pictures of pagan freedom that I cannot purge or unlove.

FIRST INTERRUPTION

I HAVE SAT HERE LONG with the pen poised over parchment and now interrupt my own history to describe events taking place in the present. One of the elder nuns, Terrech, who is blood sister to the remaining elder, Luirrenn, died in the afternoon when rain was pelting my back as I worked in the garden. I was called upon to sit with her as she took her last breath but was too late to do so. Still there was peace in her face and her eyes were closed by her own effort before death. And so we were eighteen, and a new nun, a strange woman who had been waiting in the settlement adjoining the convent, has joined Saint Brigit's order to make us nineteen again. She is very young, perhaps half my own age, and has a silken complexion and large eyes that have the color of a blue cloth left in the sun for many days. When she came to the doors, she shed her own clothing as though it were made of thorns and thistle. Naked, she knelt and kissed the hand of each sister, lingering long with her lips on our skin, so much rougher than hers for our work in the gardens and around the fires. Her hair is well combed, falling straight in oiled bands that are the color of oak bark. She keeps her eyes always wide as though in fear or in shock, even when her trembling lips are smiling. The other nuns touch her skin as though feeling linen at a fair. We are all of us compelled to act as mother to her, fondling her as one would a child. We implore her to speak, but she says little and only in whispers. She drops her head as though ashamed of words she will not let pass over her tongue or ashamed of the defect or spell that has taken the fullness of her speech away. She is like a pet come to us from another world. There are even contests between nuns as to who will sit next to her and put bread between her lips.

Much is speculated about this new sister. I say she is mad and would in other circumstances be coddled as a hopeless idiot. Others say she is the daughter of a chieftain, or she is a saint. I have seen pictures of saints in manuscripts and understand only that there is a round light that shines behind their heads, that they have performed acts of transformation, and that they are dead. There is no round light behind this new nun's head, I have heard of nothing she has transformed, and she is not dead. But I am an ignorant sinner, still tainted by the ways taught to me by a *túath* of pig raisers.

I hear her now as I have heard her every night, whispering outside my own *clochan* so that at first I thought a secret message was being spoken to me by the stones themselves. Then I stepped out into the cold darkness, and though the wind stole the hood from my head and masked my face with my own hair, I saw this new sister running into her *clochan,* which neighbors my own. She speaks to something I cannot see, and I have just heard a wail come from that place, so strange as to sound like a cry of both ecstasy and horror. I wonder if I should see that she is not harmed or taken by worms. But I dread diverting myself from my work and resent any madness or weakness that compels me from my writing. For do we not all have reason to choose weakness, and is it not our duty to resist it, or the world would be full of mewling and burdensome souls? I have often seen that the rich, though they have more meat than the poor, are yet weaker. For the poor can thresh flax from pink to gray light though their hands bleed with cuts while the rich will wail for a physician.

Her name is Sister Aillenn. I think she is from a noble family and used to the attention of captives serving platters of meats and cheeses. I think also that she has bad dreams caused by the *corpan fedilfas** we are sworn to endure. Indeed, my mother said that an empty stomach at night is entered by mischievous spirits who take the soul through unpleasant adventures as though pulling a child's cloak through the wind. I will advise Sister Aillenn to desist from her self-inflicted and arrogant suffering and take some *tanag*† from the *im noin*‡ to keep in her *clochan* for the evening, as many of us do to quiet the stomach and bind the bowels. God forgive us, but we are women who enjoy food more than hunger. Many of us come from *túath*s where

---

Corpan fedilfas: denial of food to the body for spiritual discipline.
†*Tanag:* hard cheese.
‡*Im noin:* the one meal served at monasteries, in the afternoon.

[15]

only a fool or a dying man would push cheese away. God help Sister Aillenn, whose wailing comes up again like a mourning wind, calling through the stones of my *clochan* and making my candle falter.

We are all wilted because it has rained four days and nights. I have asked Sister Luirrenn, our elder, if I could transcribe the story of Noah in order to learn the lessons of unceasing rain before having to live through them. I told her that I fear drowning in one of the puddles that grows outside my door. Sister Luirrenn glanced at my work, noticing that I did not have any text open from which I copied. She asked if I had finished transcribing the lessons of Saint Augustine. She herself used to confess a dislike of his chastising discourses, but now assumes her role of elder, more so since she now competes without her sister with the abbot, a man who came last season with his monks to occupy our convent. I say that he tries to rule it, but Luirrenn says, "He is a learned brother here to share the blessings of Brigit." But Sister Luirrenn's criticism of my work is sharp since his arrival, and I do love her so that I am loathe to anger her. Her eyes dance inside the wrinkles of her aged face, even as she scolds. She said, "It is a blessing that the abbot has too much business to look at the scratchings of an aging and unremarkable nun." She patted my cheek with playful scolding with her bent and bloated fingers that can no longer do transcriptions, and she said, "You are blasphemous and waste parchment."

When Sister Luirrenn speaks I often ignore her words

and instead speculate about the adventure that took her front teeth. Many of the women here have had thorned beds to lie in and mysterious sorrows. We soothe ourselves sometimes by clinging one nun to another in the dark nights or taking cheese and bread and blaming Bebo's folk. Luir-renn is, I confess, sometimes mocked by a sister who black-ens her own teeth to imitate the void in our elder's mouth. Sister Luirrenn hides her mouth with her hand more since the abbot has come with his monks. And the arrival of the dying infant has increased the damage to her smile.

In the second day of rain, a gray woman came with a half-dead infant to the doors of the chapel. She wanted to leave it as a sacrifice to Saint Brigit. There is much confusion among the laypeople about the new rituals and their mean-ing. When I told her that we did no sacrificing here, she handed the infant to me and said, "I cannot watch another die." This she repeated three times, so as to be heard in all realms. She then went away, hiding her face with her hair. I have since given the child over to the goatherd to see if it will be suckled by one of the goat mothers. The child, who is a boy, will no doubt be dead by dawn tomorrow, and that is why I did not hold him long against my heart. In the con-fession of faults tomorrow I will say that I am a coward. But my unwavering love is now given only to Our Lord Jesus Christ, for those whom I loved that were mortal left me in painful grief. I will also say in the confession of faults that I wanted to box the ears of Sister Aillenn, whose dramas of delicate weakness enrage me, for I was never allowed to be

[17]

weak though I was small. There is no round light behind my head; God forgive me, I sometimes enjoy rage. Neither do I have the character of the martyr, for I love comfortable places where the rain is not cold and the meals are not meager.

[2]

Concerning the history of my family: my mother, Murrynn, married my father, Clebd, because she had finished with another husband, who had trembled when she went wild and who had not given her children. He still lived in the *túath* and was greatly respected for his ability to tan and cut pigskin. I was fond of him and often wished that he were my father, because he smiled easily with large teeth and worked from pink light to gray light without complaint. My mother spoke of him with respect but did not object when my father ridiculed his lack of wit and scorned her for having lain with him.

I did not admire my own father, which is a sin I am told. I did all my work to please him because my mother's eye always turned to his face. I never received praise from Clebd. He was busy with anger concerning many things, which took him to the well where men talked and planned the *túath's* cultivation and livestock. My father also had business with the chieftain and his sons concerning the use of land and the breeding of fine horses, even though in our *túath* the chieftain was the only one who owned horses or cattle. But I do not remember my father ever working at a trade beyond conversation. He was a fearful person with thick forearms, yet weaker in character than my mother. The other women in the *túath* chided my mother for her deference to my father, and she told them to take him to their beds and see if he did not warrant pleasing. My mother had strong legs and many men who would have been her husband.

Since my father gave me no praise, I tried many methods to obtain the praise of others. And so I began the practice of showing my breasts to the boys who came to use my father's boat to fish the lake. Everyone in the *túath* knew that Clebd was not going to use the boat on any day, although failure to return it by dusk caused him to stroll heavily to the well to make promises of punishment. He discussed the matter in dark terms with the other men there, who leaned on the stones and chewed at straws with the sweat of their own work still falling down their cheeks. He was regarded as a fool but respected in part because he was my mother's husband. I did not fear that my father would strike me, because although I had become a strong young woman, my reputation as a weakling and my small frame exempted me from blows others routinely received both in anger and in games.

I did not want to anger my father. I wanted to please him in order to elevate myself in my mother's eyes. I also believed that if my father were pleased, it would be as though a spell had been broken and he would be transformed into someone noble. I did not, however, want to be a wife as my mother was. I began to think with painful concentration about the life that I would lead and the talents I had. I could not be a warrior unless horses were made smaller and weapons lighter. Though they are fine to see, horses frighten me because they are large and weak minded, which is a dangerous combination in horses, men, and gods. As I have said before, I admired the *aes dána,* especially those who had great knowledge and skill with words. I disliked mundane chores, which I did not imagine the druids had to endure, such as feeding the pigs and gathering and sorting the seeds we ate. A day's work was often consumed in one meal eaten by people too weary to know what was in their mouths. There was no connection in my mind between the thoughts I enjoyed and the mud constantly caked between my toes or the biting fleas in my clothing. The privileged druid was given food and shelter in exchange for his knowledge of rituals, laws, and magic. An *ollam** was pampered as though he were a king's son, and he had no need to fight with sword or tame a stallion.

Whoever reads these accounts must think that I suffered from the sin of sloth and wanted nothing more from my vocation than an exemption from hardship. But consider that to become a druid one must be schooled for at least nine years while learning the two hundred and fifty primary stories and the one hundred secondary stories. There are still druidic schools in existence, though they are severely challenged by the Christian priests. God forgive me, I do

---

**Ollam:* the highest form of druidic bard.

not wish to see the extinction of these old ways of knowing, for I do believe that there is still value in acknowledging the spirit in a tree and understanding how to disarm an enemy with words. Rather than seeing a contest between druid and Christian, I see a kinship between stone chapel and stone circle. One encloses and protects the spirit; the other exposes it and joins it with the elements. In both of these places we conjure the powers that affect and transcend us. We remind ourselves, in both places, that we need oats and milk, but we also need what we cannot see or put in our food bowls.

While throwing husks to my family's pigs and scratching at the bumps the fleas made on my skin, I waited for my call to the knowledge of what isn't seen. I encouraged rumors that I already had certain powers, such as the ability to turn a stone to dust by breathing certain words onto it, though I confess now that I had none. I waited for one of the druids who attended the chieftain to take me as an apprentice, for I had reached *aimsirtogu*.* As I waited, I distracted myself with the powers girls wield over boys and which Saint Patrick and Saint Augustine consider sins responsible for the fall of all mankind. I have read and transcribed our bishops' rules that say women must not try to be attractive to men but must scorn the qualities in themselves that cause men to fall from grace. It has puzzled me that men, who claim more and more authority over women, show such fear of those whom they call weak. Perhaps they

---

Aimsirtogu: the age of choice: seven for a boy, fourteen for a girl.

are hoping that women will come to believe that they need to be protected and dominated, but I cannot imagine any woman being so foolish. I wonder if Eve's seduction of Adam was the result not of evil moral frailty but of her restlessness. Perhaps Adam was more easily amused and satisfied than Eve, who wanted more than the life of a child in a pretty garden. I do not mean to blaspheme, only to show an understanding of the scriptures from my own faults. From the time of my first woman's bleeding, I suffered from a restlessness I could not understand or cure. Frequently I wondered if I did not belong in the Glen of Lunatics.

The boys who came to use my father's boat praised my breasts, which were small but well rounded. The boys who came to use my father's boat wanted to touch my breasts or to pretend to suckle, and I saw no sense in this until I came to know Giannon the Druid, and then the things said to me by the boys who came to use my father's boat seemed desirable and compelling.

I had known two druids before Giannon. One was the master of the ritual of laws and was called upon to make a judgment in the case of thievery or murder. The other was consulted on matters of agriculture and fate that needed thorough knowledge of the calendar and the movement of the stars. Both also knew some medicines, but my mother knew the plants more fully. These two druids and other travelers passing through our *túath* told various stories of druidic miracles, but I never myself saw a druid summon lightning or bewitch a man by whispering against a straw and casting it at him. But when a certain darkness, such as a black fog, traceable neither to smoke nor to cloud, came over us, the people said that this was a druid's trick. Stories even tell of battles fought between the druids and Saint Patrick in which each man summoned the source of his magic. Patrick was always victorious, and the druid was mangled in some way, his skull usually being crushed by the power of God as summoned by our first saint.

I had heard of Giannon the Druid because he came sometimes to advise the chieftain and was a master of words and histories. Once when I was holding my little sister by the wrist and striking her leg with a wooden spoon, as my older sister had done often enough to me, I raised my eyes and Giannon was there, as though having created himself from the air. He glared at me with eyes the deep brown color of the Pool of Remorseful Deeds, where shamed men drown.

When he saw me beating my sister's leg, he did not ask a question, but I felt the need to answer one. Pointing to the whimpering child with the spoon, I said, "She has disobeyed me," for she was in the habit of biting, which I did not like. Giannon took the spoon and tapped me lightly on the head, as though the spoon were a yew stick and he were making a spell. He smiled, and I saw that his teeth were good. Then he strode off with a peculiarly erect posture and long gait. His brown cape swung back and forth slowly. Giannon had hair the reddish brown color of oak leaves on the edge of winter. Beardless, he had a profusion of eyebrows, unruly and humorous, which he seemed to comb outward for whimsy. His fingers were long, and I felt that he had once, perhaps as recently as that morning, been a tree, thick branches raised like arms, leaves like the tatters of a cloak. He well liked hurling and had a reputation at the fairs for winning many competitions. I have felt his arms and know that they were strong.

That night I dreamed that I showed my breasts to Giannon and that they grew large in his hands. When I asked my mother what his powers were, she told me that his greatest power was to dispel merriment in others. But she said also that he could take words out of people's mouths and turn them into marks that he put on stones or leather as a man makes a diagram of his home in the dirt with a stick. She said that he could then read these marks at a later time; these marks could be read by another man even years after the one who made them was dead. Then, the one who was reading would hear the exact words of a man long dead and turned to dust. This began the period of my life which I call the Breathless Times, in which I connected the power of conquering death by using these marks with my desire to take my cloak off and lie down beside Giannon. I felt the possibility of transcendence using both my body and my mind, not yet understanding the concept of a soul as something that needed the intercession of a Christian priest.

The immortalizing power of words possessed my spirit like a voice in a madman's ear. Whereas I saw neither metamorphosis nor magic swords in my future—things that seemed remote and exceptional—I became sick with a desire for Giannon's knowledge and his admiration. I asked the world around, above, and below to give me the power to turn a man's voice into permanent marks and to free me from every obstacle to this power. I left sprigs of holly and raven's feather at the pool and sacred trees, asking that Giannon, whose face had strong bones, be my teacher.

At that time my *túath* had heard little of the Christians except at the fairs where the tonsured men spoke of the hero Jesus and showed the people improvements in plowing and husbandry. The monks were gaining a reputation for new methods and tools that made certain tasks easier. They brought plants from Britain that grew well in thirsty ground, and they asked only that the people who loved the plenitude these improvements gave participate in the recitation of phrases that the monks taught, such as the declaration of one's belief in the three gods in one. Our lives were harder then than now, for we had to labor hard to eat a little. We did not understand the benefits of fasting for spiritual reasons; fasting was nothing other than extreme hunger imposed on us by the absence of food. In some years the elderly and the infants died before their time because of hunger. To improve our lives and reap bigger harvests with new instruments and methods, what did it matter to alter our rituals and prayers to please our benefactors? We did not forsake our own spirits, which still lived in the trees and pools no matter what we proclaimed to the monks. We believed that the spirits of our land were permanent elements, like air and water. They had no need to be jealous if we made new sounds in praise of new heroes. The man thousands of miles away who had, it was said, defeated death for those who followed him, did not threaten the spirits who formed themselves into oak and yew. Like the tree on which Our Lord Jesus Christ was sacrificed, they and all the plants and animals and elements had a part to play in all adventures and revelations. It is no mystery that the Pelagians—those Christians who taught that all things are part of God and therefore good—found an easy welcome in this land where each twig is divine. And I am sometimes sorry that Patrick was sent to rid us of those heretics. God forgive me if I blaspheme. I am humbly recounting the events as they occurred before my understanding of the Church's merciful authority. Even now, like the Pelagians, I do not understand a jealous God, for if He made all things, then any form of worship that protects His creations and is not destructive or cruel to them must please Him. But I swear that I am not a Pelagian.

The people of many *túath*s to the north of my own allowed the tonsured men to show them a better way to harvest barley and breed horses. In such times, the raiding between *túath*s lessened, and in Tarbfhlaith we continued to be pagans but enjoyed a period in which none of our people were found dead in their fields with their pigs stolen. The people who listened to the tonsured men asked many questions, and the druids who attended the chieftains in those places debated with the monks. They asked, "On what kind of a tree was this hero Jesus sacrificed?" And the monks often answered, "It was the yew tree," which they knew was sacred to the druids, who made their staffs and wands from the yew tree. Now they make the ancient wells and standing stones into Christian relics, attributing their powers to saints. I do not quarrel with this practice, for I believe that which is sacred does not care by what name it is called. But I often wish that I did not know history so well so that I could believe more thoroughly in the Christian rendition of our landscape. Knowledge often spoils devotion.

Those in the eastern parts of this land, who first knew Our Lord Jesus Christ through the Pelagians, were told by the tonsured men to lay down that doctrine as though it were boiling poison. For it was spoken by a heretic who did not understand the sacred status of priests. These debates were not known to me when I lived in Tarbfhlaith, but only after I came here to serve Saint Brigit and transcribe the scholarly writings of the church. Now I know that Saint Patrick came to this land to make certain that the Christians here put down and renounced Pelagian ideas, which were treasonous to the pope and all bishops, saints, and priests who must protect the souls of the ignorant. Saint Augustine of Hippo revealed the Pelagians as heretics and saved Christians from notions that damn their souls. This is as I have read it. But in the days of my youth these matters were remote. My *túath* remained un-Christian, and my aim to become a druid was not challenged with religious arguments.

*Unde autem audenter dico, non me reprehendit conscientia mea hic et futurorum.**

---

*"But for this reason I boldly say my conscience does not rebuke me, neither now nor about future things."

[28]

SECOND INTERRUPTION

THE SKY HAS STOPPED RAINING, but the dew is heavy still and frosts the ground until the time for our meal. Our footsteps fall hard on the ground and the sun is small. I have put more cloth around my feet in order to travel about the abbey and its gardens. I asked about the infant who was brought to our convent and have learned that he is dead. The goatherd seemed not interested in the child's fate and gave the little corpse to me in soiled blankets. The bundle was so light that I had to unravel it to be sure a soul was there. And so I saw the unfortunate infant, blackened by the worms that diseased him. I spoke to Sister Luirrenn, who went to the houses clustered around our abbey to find the mother, but could not. We have all nineteen sisters debated as to how to bury the infant; several do not believe it right to put the unbaptized soul in consecrated ground, and since we have no *ceallurach,** Sister Luirrenn said that we should bury it in the garden. She is our elder, and so that is what we did. The garden is unkempt since the last rains, full of unwanted ten-

---

**Ceallurach*: cemetery for unbaptized children or suicides.

drils and grasses. Though the cabbages love the water, there are herbs that have drowned. Sister Aillenn wept and shivered as though standing in a frigid wind, whispering that the child would bloat because the ground was so well soaked. She begged Sister Luirrenn to let her pile stones upon the little grave and erect a cross made of yew branches. Sister Luirrenn saw no harm in this and allowed it. Sister Aillenn's skin seems made of white wax. I stare at her often and think of beauty wasting, like a perfect apple lying on the ground, which will rot before it can be tasted. But beauty and perfection do not guarantee grace and fulfillment and are always sacrificed. Life itself seems a ritual of sacrifice, and the world the altar on which plants and animals lay their own lives for the sustenance of others, and on which we lay our youth, our well-being, our loved ones, and finally our lives. I am an ignorant woman who has sacrificed all of these things but the last, and cannot say for whom or what I perform this unrelenting ritual.

In working close beside Sister Aillenn on the infant's grave, I noted that her hands tremble and she has cuts as though an animal had made marks on her neck. These mortified me, and I was angry when she seemed uninterested in her own wounds. I asked her if she were weak, and when she answered that she was, I told her to go and get *copog phadraig,** which women commonly use after their full moon time. She said then in whispers that plant gathering

---

*Copog phadraig: common plantain, used to return strength after blood loss.

was not Christian. I told her that I go often with the women in the lay settlement and gather medicinal leaves and blossoms as well as some roots. Sister Aillenn told me, as horror made her eyes large, that I should not do such a thing and that any weakness she had was a result of her sinful nature, which only the Lord Jesus Christ through his servants could correct, as long as she did not give herself over to demons.

I do not know demons well and have never seen or heard one, for I do not hear voices, nor do I have compulsions whose origins I cannot decipher. But her words and her face made me afraid, and I thought then that demons were near. I wanted to weep for the weightless, helpless infant, who could not fend off even the smallest demon. I determined to distract myself by engaging Sister Aillenn in a theological discussion and asked her opinion on the nature and origin of demons. She answered that a woman, especially one who appears to others as beautiful, has many invisible demons surrounding her that cause people to sin. I wonder if she has taken these ideas from Saint Paul and Saint Augustine, who connect self-disgust with righteousness. Self-hatred seems to me an evil thing in itself rather than an antidote to evil. If we practice self-hatred, then the sacrifice we make of ourselves and our lives is not sacred, for it is then a gift of something we hate rather than of something that we have nurtured and loved.

As a scholar I am searching the words of Our Lord Jesus Christ, especially where He has given lessons concerning demons. I do not yet understand the interpretation of His words by Saint Paul and Saint Augustine. May God forgive me. In the Christian religion the truth seems to transform, which is to say that many scholars chastise the writings of their predecessors with revelations of new truths. I am often confused. But do not think that I am not grateful for the home I have found in the bosom of Saint Brigit, who provides me with peace and the writings of many lauded scholars.

I do wonder, however, at Saint Augustine's philosophies, because I am ignorant. I still lack understanding of his complaints against Pelagius, whose followers I knew many years ago. Is it not possible that a man may speak to God directly? Is it not possible that all that we see around us, being created by God, should be considered holy? Is it not possible that instead of original sin there is original grace? I ask these things because I am ignorant. May God forgive me. For the rituals of this place do genuinely soothe me, and the voices of the nuns as we sing the psalms penetrate all my doubts and promise a transcendence of the pain and sorrow our feet walk through each day.

Sister Aillenn informed me that the new abbot is her authority on matters of sin and demons. Her devotion to him is thorough, and I envy it, being myself sometimes weary of my sin of doubting and questioning. The abbot has no official authority over the nineteen nuns who keep Saint Brigit's flame, but he is the elder of a handful of monks who have built their own dwelling here and share the chapel. Our Sister Luirrenn speaks with the abbot but does not defer to him. He acts as *anamchara*,* as we have now been told that only men may perform this and other rites.

As we are supposed to do, the nuns and monks recite the morning hymn and thirty psalms at noon, saying together, though separated by the cloth that hangs between us in the chapel, *Deus in auditorium meum intende*.† The monks are young, and the abbot does not laugh with them or listen long to their complaints about hunger. Many who come here do not understand the kind of devotion this new god asks for. In the past in our land, suffering was something that one did not seek out but which came easily enough on its own. One sought instead both to accept and avoid suffering. We celebrated the seasons of no pain or death, the seasons when rain came at night and the sun shone during the day so that a man's wounds did not fester and stink. We sought pleasure and believed it was a blessing and not a sin. We hated pain, be it inflicted on one man by another or inflicted by unseen beings or forces we could not overpower.

Therefore, many of the young men and women of this land who come to this place because they have been told that Our Lord Jesus Christ has conquered death do not easily understand the need to feel hunger and shame in order to be given grace. Those who come here from Britain are better suited to the life of a convent, since that land was Christianized before us and by more thorough means. That

---

Anamchara: confessor or authority on cleansing the soul.
†"God come to my assistance."

is why some say that Sister Aillenn is a Briton, for she seems to love well the harshness of this life.

This evening is the twentieth in our cycle, when Saint Brigit herself comes to protect her flame. Tomorrow evening we will start our cycle again, with Sister Luirrenn tending the sacred fire, the light that must never go out. All praise to Saint Brigit, raised by druid, healer of the sick, who fed the hungry and hung her cloak on a sunbeam to dry. I pray to Saint Brigit to consider the soul of the infant. I am asking all the sisters to pray beside the little grave and add more stones. I would weave evergreen boughs among the stones and touch the cross with my lips, serving whatever gods will take the tiny soul to warmth. This damp night comes with wailing, as though the infant cries out to me, pitiful and small from its unkind chamber beneath the ground. The cloth around my feet is cold and wet and my fire is small. But I thank God that I am alive without any cough or festering sore.

[3]

I HAVE SPENT these last weeks transcribing the *Epistle* of Saint Patrick, who asks that sinners endure grueling penance with the shedding of tears. I have written his words in Latin and in the language of this land, so that the priests may read them to those who are not scholars. And who among them will not already know how to shed tears? All the tears I have shed have tasted like the skin of my mother and Giannon the Druid. I could put them in copper cups, but they are like the waters of the sea, vast and deep but unable to quench any thirst. One can only drown in such waters or take from them fish to eat. The fish in my tears are so small that only a fairy could make a meal of them.

To continue my own history, which may be of some use to other scholars and sinners, I now take up my life at the last Fair of Tailltenn before my mother's death. Here I began my apprenticeship with Giannon the Druid. He sat with other *aes dána* in the oak grove, and I went there as soon as my mother had left me to attend the council. I had anticipated his presence at the fair and so had brushed my cape and clasped it with a brooch as though I were a chieftain's daughter.

It was Giannon's habit in those days to announce, "I have news," and gather about him a crowd of people. I joined the others to watch him pull objects from his leather bag. These items had power that fascinated me. He displayed scrolls covered with marks that were dark and magical and shaped like worms in various positions. Giannon was able to look at them and speak their message. He gave out the news from places I had never seen, nor would ever see. The chieftain of a lake tribe had died, and his sons were now fighting one another for his authority. In another place, a Christian man named Taillcenn—the name the druids gave to Patrick—did battle with astrologers. Many in the crowd spit at the name of this Christian, and others had no interest in him. A woman asked if the druids' magic was greater than that of the Christians, a question I have heard asked many times since. Giannon looked at me as though I might have the answer, and I covered my eyes with my hair and looked away. I did not understand why he looked to me, since I had no knowledge of the Christians beyond rumors and the warnings given by the chieftain's bards. Giannon said to the woman, "You must get this knowledge for yourself. It is better to know than to be told."

One man, a grandfather known for his strong legs that allowed him to pull a plow as though he were two young men, requested that Giannon put down on a scroll a story he was going to tell about the passing on of his wealth of pigs to one of his kin. I came very close to watch Giannon take out a stick and a tablet coated with wax. He made marks in the wax and read them back to be sure of their accuracy as the grandfather told his story and referred to certain laws. Giannon smelled like a perfume made of wax, honey, and smoke. I rested my head against his back and closed my eyes to hear the words he spoke inside the cave of his body. Others touched his hands and stroked his face, as they did with all the druids.

I whispered into his ear my desire to learn his skills in making marks and reading them. I spoke the words that cannot be unspoken, "I devote myself to you as my teacher." I said these words three times for all the realms. He made no answer; I touched his forehead with my cheek and ran to my mother. My mother was hard with me concerning Giannon and said that I should not satisfy myself with him and should find myself another druid to be my teacher.

We stayed that night with other travelers at the fair who slept together beneath the poles and skins set up for the games. I looked often for Giannon, but he was not among the druids who drank *nenadmín** and told stories of the creatures and magic they had seen. I asked one druid, a woman with tangled hair and dark circles around her eyes, of Giannon's whereabouts, but she spat and told me that he was most likely in the woods by himself.

At dawn I wandered out into a cool fog to refresh myself after a night in the realm of dreams, still with part of my eye looking for Giannon. In the movement of a slender tree I

---

*Nenadmín: crabapple cider.

thought I saw his gesture, but he did not appear. I was finally distracted by a troupe of gleemen. The *oblaire**** called out to the early risers, those who had not been put to sleep by cider, to witness the talents of his troupe. He himself, stick thin with a forked beard, was a juggler and cleverly used clay balls that had been dyed orange. The woman with him was a contortionist and could put both her feet behind her head when seated. There were also another juggler, younger than the *oblaire,* and two young brothers, musicians. One, an idiot, played the drum, and the other played a little trumpet, making tunes and insulting noises. When the troupe began their entertainment, the younger juggler continuously tossed three daggers into the air at once as the woman carried him on her shoulder. They marched about to a noisy clatter of drum and trumpet, causing dogs to bark and leap at them. I laughed loudly with the others and forgot for a time about Giannon. If such a fair were here now, I would go to it, covering my face like a leper so as to be disguised, and watch the games and gleemen without a care. May God forgive me. I loved to watch these gleemen, whose talents gave them freedom and admiration. They seemed carefree, like the *aes dána,* but not shackled by social obligation or serious ambition. If I were to be at such a fair now, though, my laughter would become still and tears come out of my eyes, for the faces I would remember and want to see would not be there, no matter if I stayed forever to find them.

---

*Oblaire: leader or elder of a troupe of entertainers.

Soon the *oblaire* held up his long hand, the fingers like winter twigs on a large oak tree, and asked the crowd to quiet itself and the dogs. The woman bent over and dropped the young juggler on the ground, which caused the people to laugh and the dogs to bark again. She then stared at the *oblaire* with her hands on her hips and her large chest heaving like waves on an angry sea. I thought by her look that she would box the man's ears. He then gave a speech, of which, I sensed, she already knew the substance and which she did not well like. The *oblaire* walked as he spoke, making a jingling noise where bells were sewn onto his clothing. The breeze sometimes pulled the two prongs of his gray beard.

He began with a question: "Who among you has not heard of Jesus Christ the Son of God?" Several people made a gesture of pushing him away and shook their heads. Some moved on to other entertainments, for the noise had woken all the fair's attendants and a game of hurling had begun. The trumpeter blew a crude note as the juggler pinched some women in the audience on their backsides. Those still attending the gleemen laughed as the *oblaire,* sensing the tastes of his audience, abandoned his sincerity and pulled out an enormous wooden cross worn under his short jacket on a leather cord. With this he pummeled the offending trumpeter on the head as the musician ran around lifting his knees high and making the sounds of chaos on the trumpet, sounding like pigs who are being kicked. I laugh even now as I write, so that I must sound mad to anyone passing by my *clochan.* There is compassion in the gleeman's merriment, for he gives it like a gift to all who see and laugh, though they be toothless and weary from sewing and culling. Sometimes I wish the priests' sermons were touched by the gleeman's wit instead of being draped in funeral cloth.

We all laughed until our eyes were wet. And then I saw two tonsured men wearing smaller replicas of the *oblaire*'s cross stand back from the crowd and speak together with amused mouths. The *oblaire* saw them as well and, kissing the cross, returned it to its concealment against his skin. The crowd unraveled, and then I saw Giannon moving away, though I had not known he was there at all. His sleeves were pushed up and there was sweat on his arms so that I knew he had been hurling. I walked to him slowly while my heart beat like a gleeman's drum.

He turned around as though he had seen me through the back of his skull and said, "If you will be my apprentice you must not speak your own opinion for nine years. After nine years you may give judgment on one matter, and after the tenth year another, and so forth, until twelve years have passed and you have given judgment on three matters. And then, if I sanction your opinions and you have learned three hundred and fifty tales, you may call yourself a druid and pretend whatever powers you want." I stood still in front of him, waiting for his demeanor to gentle and there to be a smile on his freckled lips, but I had found the surliest teacher in all the land. I said to him, "If I have opinions I will not speak them. But I will have them." And I do not know if this was an adequate response, because a man approached him, a druid well known for his satires, and took him away by the elbow while frantically imploring his cooperation in some effort.

I soon saw my mother, who had been weeping and would not say what the council of women had discussed. She held my face in both her hands and said, "You are beautiful to look on. Always know that your face is in my eyes, daughter." She told me never to forget that I was strong, even when I had to hide my strength from those who would hate it. Then a wind came up and wove our skirts together, and I thought to myself that I wanted to leave the fair and to cling to my mother's hand and wipe the tears from her face with my own hair. I told her of the agreement of apprenticeship I had entered into, fearing that it would darken her face more to hear of my allegiance with Giannon, but she only held me closer as the wind entwined our hair, binding us more into one being.

The fair had taken on an agitated and solemn tone. A black air descended over the games and feasts. An argument between hurlers erupted, and one man pushed the other on the ground and kicked him with sickening force so that no one found joy in the games any longer. While my mother bargained with a cloth seller, I looked for the gleemen, thinking to go behind a tree and show my breasts to the younger juggler. I wanted rumor or witness to come to Giannon with the news that Gwynneve inspired lust. But the gleemen had vanished. I will remember that fair as the one at which my mother became infested with worms that attacked her abdomen and could not be driven away though I would have taken them into my own body for her. I wonder how many others had their bodies entered into by worms at the Fair of Tailltenn in the year of the tonsured attendants.

THIRD INTERRUPTION

I RECORD THIS EVENT the day after it occurred. On that day, I was tending the garden, bent over with my skirts tied, trying to ignore the terrible hunger that caused me to remember the strips of meat my mother stirred into her porridges. I visited the infant's grave and found it molested, the stones dislodged and tumbled down from the cairn. The wooden cross that Sister Aillenn had erected was unearthed and crushed, by what I cannot say, though its fury battered the cross to splinters. I called two other sisters to see the damage, and they, being frightened, sought out Sister Luirrenn. When she arrived like a storm cloud, we waited as the wind pushed our robes and the day grew dimmer and chilled. We determined that the desecration had occurred some time in the night when it had been Sister Aillenn's turn to guard the flame. Sister Aillenn was found in the chapel praying, and when told of the destruction and asked if she had heard any sounds during her watch, she threw herself on the hard-packed floor and screamed. She bit her own hands until Sister Luirrenn asked for help in returning her to her *clochan*. I noted then

[43]

that the blue of the distant mountains was the color of a sorrow that is far away but always visible.

The bestial mangling of the child's little tomb has disturbed the atmosphere of the convent and caused the abbot to speak to the whole community concerning demons. He has told us that the desecration is the work of demonic forces, drawn to the corpse because it is unbaptized. I do not sleep well thinking of this. I am frightened for the infant and for myself, for I have not been baptized, though I said that I was when I first came here almost six years ago. I am a miserable liar and beg God to forgive me, but I cannot say this in the confession of faults. I do not know why I have not done so simple a thing as to have water poured upon my head. But I am, perhaps, as wicked as King Loeguire and doomed to hell, or I am the victim of demons. I do not like to think about this matter. I have asked God to tell me in clear signs when I am to be baptized and by whom, for now it must be done in secret. But I say that whenever I determine to have the rite performed, I will feel the blood of my mother and Giannon pour over my head instead of water.

And now Sister Luirrenn has asked to see my transcription of Saint Patrick's *Epistle,* and I have given them over to her. A great wind howled as she took a codex and several scrolls with her. Before I let the door's covering fall, she turned and asked me, "Do you, little Gwynneve, still write undisciplined narratives?" I answered that I did not, which was another lie I have told this woman whose skirts I would kiss for all of eternity for taking me in when I had no shelter.

I remember well her hands lifting me up and smoothing my hair as she told me that the convent was my home and she my mother. But these lies I do not repent to the abbot, and therefore they cannot be forgiven. They weigh on me, and I know now that, though words offer limitless freedom, one can be shackled by them when they are lies, as though heavy chains around the ankles weighted each footstep.

Sister Luirrenn gently said to me that to be a scribe was to hold a sacred office. Written language, she told me, was holy; words recorded that were not the words of God or of one of his saints would burn through the parchment and create a blackened path to hell for all those who write or look at them. I did not bother to ask her about the philosophers whose Greek we transcribe and whose words came long before Jesus' eyes opened in the stable in Bethlehem. When Sister Luirrenn speaks of hell, her speech does not sound familiar, but more like the speech of the abbot, whose influence I am beginning to regret and fear. I took her hand, and feeling childish with the shame of my lies, I implored her to help me on some religious matter. I asked her if she understood how there could be both hell and the feast of heroes under the ground. Was hell below or beside the feast? Her toothless mouth trembled and she said to me in whispers, "Do not speak of the feasts of Dana or of any of those demons. Do you not understand that the old gods came from hell and pretended to be heroes?" I believe that she should be taken to the Glen of Lunatics.

During the recitation of midnight prayers, the nuns faltered as Sister Aillenn came to her place, for in the rush light we saw deep shadows on her face and neck and realized quickly that they were horrible wounds. I know that the monks on the other side of the curtain must have wondered at the interruption of the psalm and the small gasps that came instead of the Latin. I am in a state of confusion and wish that God could give me peace. Even now Sister Aillenn's moans come to me in my *clochan*. I will return to the history that I have begun, which is a distraction from the disturbances of this place.

I admonish myself and all who read this not to be ignorant on any matters of which knowledge is available. Do not be afraid of the truth, and forgive me for my weak lies.

[4]

MY MOTHER AND I walked together on the road away from the fair. We did not speak until the path became confused with a felled tree and streams of mud, and we consulted each other on the true course of the road to Tarbfhlaith. We greeted travelers who came from behind us and seemed confident in the way, though my mother hid her face when three tonsured men passed us. I wanted to speak to her of Giannon, whose smell was in the air around me like a clear smoke. But my mother's attention was not on the world around her, and she finally admitted to having a large dread. She told me that she feared that great losses were soon to come for the whole land. She said that these losses had nothing to do with drought or feuds between *túath*s, but with feuds between believers. She said, "The Christians and their tonsured messengers want to separate the souls of the people of this land from the earth they walk on." When I asked her what purpose they had in doing this, she said that there was a suspicion that a person for whom the Christians spoke—a high king, perhaps—wanted the land, and that to take the land they must first separate it from the souls of the people. I said to her, "That cannot be done. How can one's soul not be attached to what is in one's eyes and against one's feet from birth until death, like a cradle, or the arms of a mother, or one's own skin?"

She did not answer, and so I said, "There are few Christians, only a small handful, who denounce greed and vow themselves to poverty. What is there to fear? They have made protests against the cruelty of sacrifice and feud." She responded, "Do not forget that they also denounce fornication and that the few are growing. Though I do not have knowledge of what the council of men discusses, it is no doubt more full of praise for the new cultivating methods and tools of the Christians than concern for our souls." She said, "Ah, how I fear the creed that scolds harmless pleasure."

Then my mother began to disdain Giannon the Druid, as though seeing in my heart his image as I walked beside her. She said, "He is no help to his fellow *aes dána*. He denounces their magic and does not praise their rituals. He effaces his own and his religion's strength by claiming that druids have powers that any human could gain and claiming that others pretend to have powers that they do not have." I said, "But he makes marks and deciphers them." She answered, "He is dangerous because he does not hold up the old powers against the new. He denounces both." I did not want to speak more to her. But she sweetly said, "Your love for him will perhaps soften his leather heart," and she took my hand and added the words, "as you keep my heart soft, though this life can so easily turn one's heart to stone." Now I know that some of my mother's sweet words described dreams and not the life I have known. For I have learned that my love cannot heal all wounds and cannot stop death.

My mother continued her warnings in Tarbfhlaith, telling my older sister, who continually denounced all people as greedy, that this land's men were being seduced by improvements in agriculture and gold coins. She warned that any famine or drought or other disaster would be a door through which many more tonsured men would come into the *túath*s and houses of chieftains to whom they already offered riches in exchange for conversion. She said, "They will bring their stronger wheats and better horses. And what is a more powerful influence to a hungry man than a table full of bread? What is more powerful to the dying than a god who can die and live afterward, displaying his wounds as though they were stains? And what is more powerful to the wailing mother than the promise that if her dead child is prayed for to the new god, he will go to a place with no pain, waiting for her to hold him again?" I record these words so a scholar may examine their accuracy.

I tear at my own breast even now when I think that at this time I did not go with my mother often to the deep woods. I saw that she was getting weak, and I was afraid of the changes in her body. I wanted to wait every minute for Giannon. Seasons passed until the time of light green leaves came and Giannon strolled into the *túath* beneath a pack of scrolls and pottery that made a jeweled noise as he walked. Many came to see him regarding news and laws, which he knew well. When he dropped a scroll, I retrieved it. When he admired the smell of some *bairgen*,* I bargained for it and fed it to him, letting his lips touch the tips of my fingers. He journeyed on to other *túath*s, and I wanted to be more than servant to him.

In this time, Thayll, one of the boys who came to use my father's boat, asked me to be his wife. He was a good man, a cousin of the chieftain, and my father was pleased with him because already this boy was a young warrior and had fathered a son. I was his wife for a fortnight and loved well his warmth. He had sweet names for me and tickled my face with blades of grass. He praised my small body, which hid a strong spirit and could endure and match his desires. But I told him soon that I thought constantly of Giannon and the powers I wanted to learn from him. I promised Thayll that I would be his wife from time to time and would use any druidic powers I acquired to help him as a warrior. He taught me how a man and woman can give each other pleasure and tangle their limbs together. But my soul and his never recognized each other. I did these things many years ago, before I knew Christian laws.

Though I was still small and doomed to seem frail, my body was full of womanhood, and I knew its strengths. I began again to accompany my mother to the deep woods, for now she needed help in carrying her sacks. In her devotion to the rich and fertile forests, I recognized the nature of my own emotion concerning Giannon the Druid. The

---

*Bairgen: cake speckled with currants.

fertility of the woods seemed related to my own body's texture. I had the notion that if Giannon and I had our bodies opened by a warrior's blade, sweet black earth and deep red petals would fall out instead of blood and organs.

When Giannon returned, almost a half year since I had last seen him, he had become known well for a satire he told about a chieftain in a neighboring *túath*. This satire revealed the chieftain's weaknesses, including a rash on his groin, and so destroyed his authority. Giannon was now greatly praised by our chieftain. The people of Tarbfhlaith presumed that Giannon's powers were great and had expanded beyond the telling of news and recording of laws. He was therefore set upon to cure the sick.

Two young children were dying, and their parents asked Giannon for a cure, as did a man with a rancid swelling on his leg. Giannon told them that he knew no more than the cures they knew, including the plants and ritual appeals to the spirits of certain trees and pools. The people persisted, asking for spells. Giannon insisted angrily that he had none and knew of none. He said, "Perhaps the druid Cuillard, who knows of worms and poisons, can help." He said that he was sorry for their pain and that there was nowhere that he went where there was no pain. Our oldest grandmother said, "I have heard of a place where there is no pain." She said that the tonsured men had told her about such a place. Giannon's eyes and mouth drew down in weary sadness. He told me when we were alone and touching each other's fingers that people will go anywhere and to anyone who promises them a place of no pain, and that they will even forsake their own wisdom and destroy their own homes and fields for such a promise. He asked me, "What power do you want?" And I answered, "The power of words." And he told me two stories concerning the displacement of the Formorians, that ancient tribe of immortal and greedy beings.

Soon after, Giannon and I bathed in the lake, and though I hung my arms around his neck and pressed against him so that my skin touched his, he did not ask me to be his wife. But he looked long into my eyes until I thought his eyes were my own. We laughed without speaking, and I slept in the sun with my head on his chest. Time then was made of moments of thorough peace and deep agitation. His body was young and as pleasing as Thayll's to look at.

At this time Giannon gave me my first lesson in deciphering marks. He entrusted me with one of his scrolls and said, "Study this." I asked how I would begin, and he said, "I will tell you what the first line says and then you will study the marks and how they correlate with the sounds." The line he told me was *Criost ferr, fisi dia cech druí.** I asked him if he believed this, and he said it did not matter if one believed words or not, but only if one understood them and their power. That first scroll seemed to me a treasure that I was hardly able to touch without losing my breath. And now I am surrounded by scrolls, tablets, codices, and parchment that mice rummage through as though they were only dried leaves.

With my scroll in my hand I felt larger than any other

---

* "Christ is more knowledgeable than any druid."

mortal except Giannon. The apprenticeship with him had begun, and I knew that it was to be of an intimacy rarely known and never fully described. I told my mother about the scroll and watched her pass her trembling hand over it, tracing the marks with her fingers and holding on to me to steady herself. For she had begun to lie down for long times during the day. And when she spoke, it was often about the end of the world. I did not know where her wild joy had gone. I confess now that I was angry with her for her weakness. I chided her with her own stories of Mebd and Marach and other women whose strengths made them immortal heroes. But she grew thinner and quieter, and soon I found her always on her bedding.

I made it known throughout the *túath* that I owned a scroll and was learning the arts of the *aes dána*. My father ridiculed the work that I did with the scroll, and my mother was too weak to praise it in his presence. My older sister, who was the mother of two sons then, chastised me for not doing practical work and for therefore putting more burden on our infected mother. But my mother held my hand and asked that I tell her what the scroll said. She placed her polished pebbles over the marks, arranging them in triangles and spirals on the parchment. I studied the scroll on my own in the evening after brushing the floor and securing the pigs. When it was not damp or cold I took a rush light outside and worked over the puzzle of the marks. I muttered the sounds to myself, and when I identified one sound with one mark, I found that mark throughout the text and applied the sound where it occurred. In a few weeks I had deciphered many names and could see where they were re-peated in the text. Many of these marks referred to the stars, which I also studied, for the text detailed the astrol-oger's art and identified Christ as a master astrologer. I have not since heard this theory spoken and well understand its blasphemous nature. May God forgive those who misun-derstand Our Lord Jesus Christ. I wanted to see Giannon, but he did not come to our *túath,* and some said that he had transformed himself into a salmon so as to avoid his ene-mies. One man said he caught a salmon that looked at him with such disgust that he returned it to the water and de-termined it to be a druid.

When the worms' corruption of my mother's body be-came rampant, the druid Cuillard was sent for because of his healing reputation. Cuillard was a strange man to me because his skin was orange and his beard as thick as gorse. I watched him place stones upon my mother's chest and abdomen and make noxious teas for her to consume. He chewed meat and spit it into the fire, saying words that I do not remember and dare not say in this place. I asked Cuil-lard boldly about Giannon, and he told me sharply, "He has secluded himself." Giannon to me was more holy and su-perior because of his reclusive nature. I wanted to stop look-ing on my mother's wasted body and thin face and go into hermitage with Giannon as close as my own clothing to warm me. I would hide my eyes in his shoulder and smell the wax, honey, and smoke on his skin.

When Cuillard left, my mother tried to get up and do her work as though the worms were dispelled. She leaned on me as we slowly walked to the deep woods, and I began to weep heavily at having such a diminished and unhealthy being to compare with my mother, who had strolled in front of me like a sister goddess not so long before. She said, "Listen to the voices that speak only to someone who can be very quiet. The wind has a voice. The leaves have voices. The stones have voices." I said bitterly that the stones did not speak to me. My mother held me close to her, and I could feel how every physical effort made her tremble when once she had lifted me and held me. I felt then that the world was a worthless and cruel place.

Closing her eyes, my mother listened to the small ringing of water coming up from below the earth into the pool. I looked well at her face, the cheekbones grown sharp and her hair streaked with wild white hairs. Without opening her eyes she said, "You are looking at death, my little Gwynn," and I put my head down into my hands. We walked back through the woods slowly. She stopped to listen to the calls of birds and the rattle of leaves that still clung to winter branches. She said, "I still cling to the branch, but I am ready to fall. I am ready to rest." And I felt anger at her weakness again. When we were home, my mother lay on her bedding, which my sister had fattened with more reeds. My father raged about Cuillard's failure to rid my mother of the worms.

Soon my mother began to shed blood from her body through her mouth. Death was surely just outside our home, drawn by the smell of her blood. I fell on my knees and begged the earth beneath our bodies to comfort and cure her. She retched terribly and woke my little sister, who called out to her. But my mother's will, which normally drove her to her needful children, was no longer master. Something else had her body, and it was no longer hers to control. I saw in her eyes the unspeakable torment of a mother who cannot go to her child who calls out to her, and I knew it was finished. I knew, too, that she had been the only one who believed from the beginning that I was strong, and now she would be gone and no one would understand as she had. No one would remember how we had laughed at the raven who hopped on one leg and then the other, a raven we named Hopper and never failed to search for on our walks.

I sat by my mother, making my first true decision to endure and not be a coward. I wanted not to see her end, for it was ugly and not heroic. I wanted to press my eyes shut until she was the woman walking before me in the woods with her black hair and dark cloak. But I knew that I would have to live forever with what I did on that night of dying, and that if I chose to be a coward, I would have to repeat such cowardice over and over again in order to justify that it had ever occurred. And so I stayed there and held her hand, which was wet with the watery blood she had wiped from her mouth. I touched her forehead with my fingers, and I said to her that I thought she was a great woman whom many would remember. I said that I would make marks that would tell about her and would live forever. I told her that I would wait my whole life to see her again in a place that had none of this pain. The pigs snuffled nearby, and fairies as tiny as insects flew about her mouth; I waved them away with my hand. I told her, "I will stay with you." My father grabbed his hair in both fists and left the dwelling. We heard him moaning outside, and we heard also the squeal of a pig that he kicked. He left and did not return until dawn, after my mother's body had lain lifeless for a long time and I knew that she was no longer in her cold and rigid flesh.

Soon began my father's obsession with the burial of my mother. He commanded that she be buried in an unusual fashion, without any druid in attendance. He commanded that a tonsured man be fetched or created among some member of the *túath* and that a Christian burial, of which he had no particular knowledge, be performed. There was no pacifying him. Though I fed and coddled him like a child, he refused to relent in the business of her funeral. It became clear that my mother's body would either decay or be buried according to my father's intense whim. The household itself was diseased, as though the worms that had stricken my mother were in the air around us. There was a black fog there. My older sister could be consoled by nothing, getting no comfort from the idea of any burial. She screamed, "We will see her no more. We will see her no more."

My older sister and my father began to battle each other in thundering voices, and I looked on, bloated with grief. I held my little sister, who sucked her fingers and wept without sound. And finally I made a pack out of pigskin and put in it some cakes, a cup, a dagger, and Giannon's scroll. That night I secretly lay down next to my mother's body, which was covered in a shroud so delicate that my words made it flutter around her head. I whispered in her ear, "You are gone, Mother. I will see you no more as I have seen you since I was born." I wept against her hard shoulder until spittle came down my chin. Then I rose and walked straight and heedless into a night thick with mournful spells and blackened spirits. My motion then, though vague, was to take a pilgrimage to Giannon or to solitude and return to Tarbfhlaith before the next moon. I had a belief in nothing but sorrow.

*Qui crediderit salvus erit, qui vero non crediderit condemnabitur.**

And now moans Sister Aillenn, walking on the rocks outside my *clochan* and repeating in breathless whispers the Kyrie Eleison as though expressing the inconsolable sorrow that lives in my memories, though the birds continue to fly through the sky with the joy of wings.

˒

---

*"He who believes will be saved, but he who does not believe will be condemned."

FOURTH INTERRUPTION

SISTER AILLENN HAUNTS ME. She is the old land of beauty and chieftains, whispering the Latin prayers as though to transform her soul from its sinful pagan nature. I want to take her hand at times and run with her far, far to the deep woods, so that branches whip our faces and briars tear our skirts, and we run so far and so swiftly as to be transformed into deer, leaping free of any doctrine but the doctrine of pools and grass. But these are dreams, perhaps put into our minds by demons. For Sister Aillenn has told me that, as she was asleep, Satan attacked her violently. She said, "He fell upon me like the stump of an ancient oak, embracing me with the dead roots, and I was completely paralyzed."

I have recently transcribed the image of Satan as a crushing boulder in the writings of Saint Patrick.

The grave of the infant has been repaired, but I have since noted frantic claw marks in the dirt, as though some beast has still been trying to dig up its buried obsession. Now the grave is well covered with stones and there is no cross above it, so that it looks like a pagan cairn. And in this I find some comfort.

Brigit, whose kindness relieves pain,
Brigit, who feeds the hungry,
Brigit, whose poetry soothes mortal sorrow,
Be with me now like a mother.

There has been a sickness passing through the convent, causing pains in the stomach. We have had a Christian man who knows medicine come to manipulate our limbs and give us cultivated herbs. These are times when Saint Brigit's kindness is sorely needed. I lie down upon my bed close to the little fire and pray for some comfort, since the cold causes the pains to grow sharper. I cannot write this day any more and cannot go even to the chapel to sing the psalms. May God forgive me.

[5]

THE VOICE OF MY MOTHER was silent, though I listened for it always. Only when I stopped begging and waiting for it, much later than the time I am telling of here, did I hear it in breezes and owl calls. I wanted no other magic but her human presence. I would have traded all gods and spirits for the lowly carnality of one beloved woman. But I did not know with whom to make such a bargain. The universe was as silent as my mother.

I was afraid, too, of my own mortality. Death had come into my life and now knew me. I could not hide from it any longer. One day I would die, afflicted with worms or drowned or the victim of blows or blade. I received comfort then by looking at the stars, whose infinite depth the night I left Tarbfhlaith hinted at a large magic in which the birth and death of humans were small things. Some stars were round like distant suns, and others were made of shining white mist and wound like a road between the constellations. But I could read no message in the stars and wondered what could be deciphered there by a druid who could translate the night sky.

And what message would I have wanted from the stars that night when I wandered motherless for the first time in my life? What message would I want the sky to tell me on any night? That I am loved? That I am protected? That something understands my efforts though they fail? That the sky is a curtain behind which all that we long for waits, all the dreams we mourn that are held in the arms of the dead, who wait and whisper like children in a game of hiding? That if I have faith I will be embraced by an understanding that is complete and blissful? Perhaps if one stops looking up at the stars and looks instead at this world, the messages we need would be there and the gods could tend to larger matters than one tiny person's sorrow.

I did not know and still do not know what message would give me the greatest comfort, for all signs in the end seem to be desperate interpretations by those who must have some explanation for the pain of living. Were I to enter a copse of yew and oak and see in the center an *ogham,* * what would I be most happy to see written there, protected by the moss of ages? The Ten Commandments admonish me to behave a certain way, and for what purpose do I follow them? I am promised the Kingdom of Heaven, but what then will I do forever in the Kingdom of Heaven, unless there is a bliss that I do not understand, that is eternal without being tedious? When I ponder eternal life, I sometimes imagine a time when I will be sorely weary of endlessness.

Ogham: stone on which words and marks were carved, sometimes to mark a grave or place of significance.

The idea that every movement, every vision goes nowhere but to an endless space of more movements and visions seems almost horrible. Then I prefer to think of the variety of lessons and the series of beginnings and endings inherent in incarnation into other bodies; or of the peace of ceasing to have thoughts and my body becoming crumbs that feed all who live after me. But believing one thing rather than another does not make that thing the truth.

The night I left my mother's corpse and my *túath*, I walked in the direction of the next *túath*, which I had never seen but knew to exist through the ferny woods to the west. I knew that it was two days' walk away from Tarbfhlaith and that Giannon lived near it. I slept against a hill where old leaves had collected. It was a cold night, but the hill stopped the wind and the leaves covered me like a well-woven blanket. Just before dawn, I ate some of the *bairgen*, which I had wrapped in cloth and put into my pack. Shivering, I thought then of returning to my own *túath* and resuming life as Thayll's sometimes wife and as my father's helper as I continued to study and meet with Giannon when he came to Tarbfhlaith. But I could not yet go back. I was someone else; I had been transformed and could only pretend to be the Gwynneve that my *túath* knew. I thought to wait until I knew who Gwynneve now was and then return.

My plan was to find Giannon, who would allow me to grieve and who I believed understood what my grief encompassed. I would continue to learn the stories, for I had three hundred and forty-eight more to memorize. As I wandered through the deep woods, I passed the farthest place I had gone to with my mother. I stopped there and sat beside the pool where she had carefully washed pebbles and chewed leaves. The place became still and I felt her there; even the water did not trickle, the leaves did not flutter, and no birds sang. I could almost see her, bent over with passionate concentration and then looking up to see me and smiling. Thunder drummed in the distance. In one breath I grew afraid of my grief. A spirit tempted me to slide into the pool, soaking my cloak and hair and sinking to the bottom where the spirit's sad sisters would clutch at me and help me to drown.

I ran from that place, weeping and cursing the vines and branches that whipped my face. When the sun was overhead, I stopped again, in a clearing with yellow clouds and blue sky as its roof, and I did not know where I was. I was confused and drained of calm reason. In terror, I sank to the ground and looked at the unfamiliar configurations of trees and colors and land around me. I muttered over and over to whatever invisible spirits I entertained there that I was lost. I sat down to tame my breath and an unusual peace overtook me. There was still the low drumming of thunder somewhere to the south, but a bird twittered over and over in a tree nearby, its lack of concern a satire of my panic. I recognized my terror as a child's terror about being lost and not seeing one's mother again. I understood that I did not have to fear that any longer because my mother was dead. I was lost to her and she to me, no matter where I was, so that now I was free to be anywhere without hoping and waiting for her protection.

This is a strange philosophy. But it provided me with a peaceful grief and an ability to walk forward, assuming that I would either live alone, according to my own wits and knowledge of the woods, or I would find others who could clarify my intended direction. I would return to Tarbfhlaith with some authority with which to gain respect and purpose. I longed for Giannon, but did not believe that haste would increase the certainty of finding him. He often traveled and could be in any *túath* in the land. I lay down and slipped into a half world, neither seen nor dreamt, where logic becomes one shape in an intricate geometry with many heights and depths. In such a half world, a man lies frozen on his bed, believing he must rise in order to restore his head to his body with clay. He does not question his certain logic until he is fully awake and then may laugh at himself. In such a state, I believed that if I spoke to Giannon, repeating three times each phrase, he would hear me wherever he was. And my teacher in this effort was the bird that continued to sing the same three notes over and over.

I awoke to the liquid trills of another bird, a dusk bird, and rose quickly to my feet as though the sound of its song had pinched me. The world was darkening, and I saw in the distance the orange lights of fires. I walked toward them, not knowing their size or origins. If fairies were luring me to some enchantment, then I would fall into it; if the fires signified a *túath*, then I would welcome them and find company or death by a warrior's angry ax, thus giving some man an easy entry into a tale of enemy killing. I wound a leaf around my finger and wished that whatever creatures I found were friends to the people of Tarbfhlaith. I was not well acquainted with the enmity between various *túath*s, which in fact changed according to warriors' whim.

As I moved toward the flames, I saw that they were huge in size. There were dozens of fires. I waited in a patch of brambles and tried to understand what I saw. Each fire was three times the height of the men in hoods and cloaks who were coming and going between the roaring hills of flame. Animals, some small such as hares and some big such as wolves, ran from the flames; some of them were on fire, and I could not look at them but had to hear their screams. It seemed as though an entire valley was on fire, and the black smoke eclipsed the first stars. I wondered if I were not seeing another realm, where worlds were created and destroyed by humans who served angry gods by stoking the fires. For what deity they did this work I could not say. I cowered in the forest, squatting and holding my knees, afraid to move.

The fires burned all night, and I left that place, though I might have left comfort and help. I walked northward, keeping the flames always to my left. I was not long away from them when I saw the black silhouette of a circling wall and was glad to find a *túath,* though I had no knowledge if the people there were friend or enemy. Soon I came upon a herdsman and shyly let him know that I was a wanderer and an apprentice to a druid. He showed no fear of strangers and shared bread and cheese with me though my hands were dirty. I here give thanks and praise to this herdsman, whose name I do not know but whose generous hands I have never forgotten, and to his good goat. How small an act of kindness can be to the giver while being great to the receiver. This man knew of Giannon and could tell me in which direction his home was. But I was interrupted in my journey by those gleemen whom I first saw at the Fair of Tailltenn.

FIFTH INTERRUPTION

IN THE CONFESSION OF FAULTS I will have to mention my arrogance, which grows as I transcribe the writings of Saint Patrick. Perhaps it is not of importance to his sainthood that his Latin is ragged and I must correct it as I copy. But now I often remember the stories told to me by Giannon about Patrick, whom the druids called Taillcenn, a man slow to be merry. He laughed at no satire, especially those that told about him.

There is the story of his journey across the sea to Britain. He came upon a set of rough boatmen and asked them to take him in their boats to his destination. I do not know if at this time Patrick knew that he was a saint, though he had declared himself bishop and everyone in the land had heard of him and knew his appearance. The mischievous men told Patrick that they would take him in their boat only after they had suckled him, and they showed him their bare chests. Blasphemed, Patrick refused, claiming that as a Christian he could not perform such an act. The men laughed so hard that they bent to the ground and then slapped Patrick between the shoulders as though he were a cousin. The leader of the boatmen called out that if he had known that Patrick was a Christian, he would have met his demands without hesitation. He said, "Indeed, there is no fee at all for taking a Christian out of Ireland." Though this story is wicked and its truth uncertain, it gave Giannon and other druids much pleasure. Patrick himself records this occurrence as a sample of the power of Christianity.

It is hard to know the truth in the matters of saints. Some still say that Sister Aillenn is a saint because of her suffering. But if suffering makes saints, then all the people of this land are saints. When I trade cabbages with the people whose homes clutter the hillside beside the convent, I see pain in every eye. I see the woman whose husband I sat beside after he was trampled by the wild horse who runs in this region with a companion mare. I see the young girl whose brother died of lung worms; he sat on my lap while I wiped his brow, sweated from the labor of dying. I see the woman who brought her baby here to die. She hides her face with her hair and does not brush the grass from her cloak. She wanders about like the one who dreams but does not sleep. I have combed her hair and seen the scabs on her scalp. Sometimes I bring her a piece of parchment with words on it and tell her it is a blessing. Each time I see her she grasps my hand and begs that I bring the infant back to her. She is consumed by guilt, for she believes that she made a grievous error in leaving the infant with those of the new god who planted him in the ground with no thought to the heroes and gods who might have cared for his soul until it found its way to a new home.

I place my hand over her blistered lips when the abbot passes us and she is muttering about her breasts, which swell to feed an infant who is no longer able to suckle.

[6]

THESE WORDS set down the events that I carry in my mind. I give thanks for the ability of words to fix for all times the lives of the saints and the doctrines of Our Lord Jesus Christ. But here I humbly and gratefully use them to immortalize the lives of two beings whose genius and beauty have died before they were recognized. Now that I have told of Murrynn, whose voice trickles in my head, I pray that I do not die myself before I am able to set down the character of Giannon. The dead potential of my mother and my teacher is a burden that agitates me, for I cannot re-create it, only record it. Thus is the limitation of words, which only God can make into flesh. My beloved mother, whose wild joy was tempered by her calming touch, and my brother Giannon both thwarted their own genius, owing to what purpose or shame I cannot say. Perhaps it is weariness that causes the seers not to act on what they see; for whereas the wisdom of the world can be vast, it includes the many futilities. Ideas do not have legs with which to run and hands with which to craft. They are wisps of smoke floating into a universe of pain and ignorance that overwhelm the capacity of one small human body and the mind trapped inside it. My mother's devotion to a husband beneath her in wit and effort caused her own life to wither. Giannon's devotion was to his solitude. Had I known how deep this devotion was and how painful and destructive it would be, perhaps I would have stayed where the shepherd fed me. But the shepherd's chin was weak. I searched for Giannon, knowing that he was the match to my own soul and wanting his hands to know my skin.

In this search I walked for one day from the shepherd's *túath*. At dusk on that day I saw another fire in the woods, but this one I determined to be small. Still, I was cautious in approaching it and came slowly to a clearing where I found a merry sight. Five human figures were arranged in an unusual geometry around the small fire. I recognized the *oblaire* at once because of his forked beard and thinness. He was standing straight as a stick, lecturing to his fellow gleemen, two of whom lay straight as rods beside the fire. The younger juggler was upside down, with his head where his feet should have been and his feet in the air, pointing to the pale clouds. The woman sat with both legs extended outward in the air next to her ears. It was with surprise and joy that I recognized this troupe. I was glad to see a face I had seen when my mother was alive.

I came through the brush and introduced myself as a woman who had seen them at the Fair of Tailltenn. They welcomed me warmly, the woman taking me to her side to sit by the fire with her as though I were her charge. She held my head to her breast and said, "Here, then, the loss of your

mother is a poison in your body, girl, but it will not kill you."
Even when the grief was not severe, there was still a bitterness in all the food I took. When I told her that I was
now looking for Giannon, she said that he was traveling, and
she said that perhaps the poison had stricken my reason or
left me weak to the mischief of certain fairies who could
inflict me with a desire to visit such a man. I explained that
I was his apprentice, and I showed the scroll to the troupe.
The *oblaire* narrowed his eyes and said, "Giannon is a solitary man, sour and unfriendly. And like all druids, he knows
he is done for." This statement put frost on my heart, for I
did not expect to hear my mother's doomsaying from other
mouths. I said, "My mother, who is recently dead, warned
of the Christians and their ambitions." The *oblaire* did not
speak and walked away. The woman told me, "He is a Christian, a Pelagian." I did not know then what manner of a
Christian a Pelagian was, thinking them all the same. But
I was weary both from traveling and from grief and asked
no questions. I laid my head in the woman's lap and let
her stroke my hair as though I were her child. Because of
her tenderness, I stayed for a time with the gleemen in
that place.

Their lives were free and unusual, though not as privileged as the lives of the *aes dána*. At their camp they prac-
ticed their arts and brought food, which they got from the
nearby *túath* of grain growers. They spoke of their route and
the fairs they would attend. These decisions were shared
by the *oblaire*, the woman, and the younger juggler, for one
of the musicians—the drummer—was a half-wit, and his

brother the trumpeter watched over him. The drummer was like a child though his body was large like a man's. One day his shoe caught fire while still on his foot. He was thereafter tied to a tree for the night. I spent my days studying the scroll and helped my companions gather foodstuffs in the woods. We worked hard to feed ourselves and to keep a supply of dry wood in the cart for the times when it rained and when even our bones were damp. The younger juggler hunted and roasted birds, which tasted delicious to me. I became the wife of the younger juggler, whose chest hair gleamed in the morning light as though some of the strands were made of orange gold. I well liked his warmth at night.

One night during a storm I heard the half-wit howling and crying like a dog. I got up from beside the younger juggler and went to him. When I untied him he beat me so that I had to cover my head with my arms. The woman woke and wielded a large stick, striking the half-wit many times to get him to loosen his hold on me. In the morning I was unable to rise quickly from the ground. The half-wit gave me his portion of milk and wept. I had no quarrel with forgiving him, for fear and ignorance struck the blows as much as his fists. The gleemen were becoming my family, and I well love them even now, though those who still live are pagans and heretics and hidden from the punishment of the Christian bishop. I thought still of Giannon, speaking to him as though he lived inside me and dreaming of his enfolding and protecting spirit as my lifelong comfort. But I waited for the swelling and marks on my face to heal and languished in the security and comfort I had with the gleemen, who amused me well. I laughed at the trumpeter, who could mimic the voice and movements of any human or beast. I liked most his imitation of the *oblaire,* whose stern accounts of the new god irritated his friends greatly.

The *oblaire* schooled me in the Pelagian doctrines. He was devout and passionate in his conversion, which had occurred when he was a boy and his family had drowned. I listened with interest as the others snored or waved their hands for him to stop talking. But here was a man who, through neither force nor promise of increase of his stores, had turned to the new religion. It may be well for the Church to thank rather than persecute those who worship Christ though they do not worship priests, for their conversion brings them closer to the truth so beloved by the priests. But I am ignorant of these matters.

Perhaps there should be another account of the Pelagians besides those of Saint Augustine. It may be valuable to have other sources of information concerning the various heresies. The *oblaire* said, "The hero Jesus Christ has proven his power over death. He does not fight the waves with a sword, as did Cuchulain, but walks on the water without sinking or drowning. He does not rage against the worms and decay of this world, but touches a man and heals his sores. There is no fairy mischief in Christ's kingdom, nor bickering gods who promote wars. The hero Jesus offers a life without suffering, eternal life in Paradise, for God gave His grace and the hero Jesus brought the message of God's grace. This tree, this leaf, this sky are part of God and his grace. Who wants to continue this round of suffering, battles, famines, and worms? In each mote of dust there is God and His promise of Paradise."

The half-wit pressed his hands against his ears when the *oblaire* spoke these words, for he was afraid of fairies. He said that the fairies were jealous of Jesus. But the younger juggler said, "I do not see the harm in telling stories about the hero Jesus and also setting out milk for the spirits that live and play around us. Jesus is not from our land; the people of this land know its power and cannot pretend to forsake what they see and feel and hear around them every day. You can call the spirits that live in the pools and trees God's grace if you like, old man. But if Jesus were from this land he'd be putting milk out for the fairies himself." And though your skin may turn red at his blasphemy, could you not consider it and also consider such men harmless sons of their pagan mothers? I say here that I am ignorant and do not understand the persecution of the Pelagians, who love Our Lord Jesus Christ without loving priests and bishops and others who elevate themselves with the hat they wear or the staff they carry. May God forgive me.

The woman in the troupe said sharply to the *oblaire* that the Christians had new ways and that the *oblaire*, according to them, would burn forever in eternal flames that needed no wood or peat for not renouncing his ideas and deferring to the rituals and instructions of the tonsured men, who spoke to God for the lowly. I told her that I had seen these eternal flames and the men who tended them to the west. I explained that indeed they did need wood and peat. The younger juggler told me that those were not the fires of eternal damnation but fires to clear the land, set by the monks of Saint Patrick to increase the size of the sowing fields. I asked him if the spirits of the burned trees and scorched earth would flee as the flaming animals had and do mad mischief to show their rage. I was afraid then of my mother's warnings and how death had shut her mouth. I was confused as to what held power and how power was used. I regret that I am still unsure when the night is long.

I slept sometimes in the arms of the woman when I was mired in grief and loneliness. The younger juggler was small like me, and sometimes I wanted the large softness of the woman's comfort. The gleemen wanted to teach me a skill, but I could not juggle even two clay balls. I showed them the marks that I could make and how they could be kept and read. But there was no profit in this art for a gleeman; instead, there was danger in doing the work of druids without their sanction. I was therefore simply a companion to the gleemen and contributed no useful talent except in a sin I confess here. For being small and quick, I was able to enter the *túath* at night and return with what we needed to make a meal when honest attempts had left us hungry. I have confessed this transgression many times and ask God to forgive me. But even Our Lord Jesus Christ urged a man to use his talents.

I traveled with the gleemen to two fairs, confessing my hope of finding Giannon. I sorely wanted to know more words and advance my abilities to make marks. I hid my face with my hair and wandered about the games and feasts, stopping to listen to the druids. I saw tonsured men push the druids to the ground, but I saw no kin or other face known to me at either fair. I did not hear of Giannon until the coldest season, when the trumpeter and his brother returned from some honest trade in the *túath* of grain growers and told me that Giannon was there, on his way to his home. The younger juggler studied my face, and when I turned to look at him, I could not speak. I knew that it was a mean season for a wife to leave a man, for he would feel the cold sharply, but I prepared to go, packing scroll, cup, and dagger. When I was ready to part from the gleemen, the younger juggler had gone to hunt wild pigs, taking the half-wit and his brother with him. I walked northward heavily, telling myself the two stories I knew of the Formorians so I would not feel the whole of my regret. I was still weak in attaching myself to mortals and had not yet learned to avoid the sorrow of separation.

SIXTH INTERRUPTION

SAINT BRIGIT, mother of God, sweet mother whose skin shines with grace and light, be with me. I have guarded your flame this night, and as the sun comes up in heather blossom clouds, my duty is done. I am filled with love and gratitude for your constant presence and protection. Terror sat in my empty stomach this long night, and I am glad that I have done my duty. Though my face was heavy with weariness and the rain made a steady lulling noise, I did not sleep but stayed vigilant. Was it you, beloved Brigit, who rattled the shutters as though you were the wind? The noise becomes so large in the empty chapel, lit only by your flame. Was it you who danced like a dark maiden against the walls to soothe my loneliness? For I confess that I am very lonely at times.

Once when the night was still and the rain gentle, I heard knocking and a voice calling out, and I was afraid to move. I have been infected with thoughts of demons, and though in the day I do not think them solid, at night I can imagine their open mouths and twitching fingers. I pray to have no fear and wish, dear Brigit, that you or Our Lord Jesus Christ would come before me in a form so clear that I could not doubt it. My doubts oppress me, and as I write my own insignificant history, in order to set down events and ideas concerning great changes and suffering, these doubts grow like thistles and sting me. I feel now another power of words, which is to reveal things to the very person who writes them. And I am afraid of what is revealed and the emotions the words dislodge and send tumbling down upon my head. Dear sweet Brigit, whose eyes are love and whose touch is healing, comfort me and let me know what is true.

[7]

GIANNON'S HOME was a configuration of branches, stones, and mud. A dome and a shed of these materials leaned against one another like old drunken warriors at a banquet. All around these structures was a variety of grasses, blossoms, and bushes that I had never seen before. Drying herbs, jars on tethers, and staffs of yew and oak hung on the sides of his dwelling so that it reminded me of Giannon himself when he traveled beneath a tangle of druidic accessories. The clearing with its gardens and dwelling was empty of human life, though a ragged gray wolf scampered into the woods from there. Some might say that the wolf was Giannon transformed, but I only had the sense that the wolf was hungry and weak, for the past winter had been fiercely cold.

I entered the dwelling and found the inside also strung with dried plants, jars, and staffs. There were shelves on which a chaos of boxes and jars sat along with feathers and scrolls and dust. The only furnishings were a table, a small bench, and a bed made of straw covered with the skins of bear and fox. More scrolls, codices, and tablets sat upon these furnishings, as though the originals had multiplied in some orgy when their master was away.

I walked carefully through this strange chamber, afraid that all of Giannon's belongings and the dwelling itself were capable of collapsing into a dusty pile of rubble. And I believed that a druid's dwelling could likely be set with spells from which I would emerge transformed into a beetle or bee. I waited for Giannon outside, until the world grew dim and I could see wolves running along the tree line beyond the small clearing in which Giannon's home nested. Finally I saw Giannon approach as a moving and dark form emerging from the trees. I stood, so I would not startle him, and he nodded and entered his dwelling without speaking my name. I waited to follow him, and when I did, I found him in his bed and a wax candle lit upon the table. I lay down beside him. That night we warmed each other but did not become husband and wife. And in the morning when I awoke he was laboring devotedly in his garden. As I watched him there, bending to disappear into the reeds and emerging again as from a lake of grasses, I felt cold, for he had no words nor glances for me. I remembered and grieved the death of my mother as though it had occurred the night before. I was a child, with a child's fear of loneliness.

I was old enough then to be a mother myself but had used the ways now outlawed by the Church of keeping a child from growing in my womb. These ways have been banished and so violently punished that the knowledge is lost to most women and unspoken by those who remember. The Christians say that a man must choose his wife and plant his seed in her and know that what he sows is his and not another man's or the result of a covenant between a woman and a demon. These are the new laws. But then I was a pagan, and I had not wanted any child but Giannon's and thought it right to create a human being from my own desire. Then I was pagan and believed that the only demons who could plant a seed in a woman's womb were the men who drank ale and mistook their daughters for their wives. May God forgive me for my ignorance.

For many weeks I slept beside Giannon and worked beside him at the table, learning new marks. But though he held my hand in both of his to keep me close, though he touched my face to show his affection for it, and though he laughed with me, he did not lie on me or push himself against me. I spoke with him about my sorrow and longing for my mother; I told him that I had had two husbands before him. There was no secret that I did not tell and that he did not understand. And he began the process of showing me every skill that he knew, holding no secret to his bosom, having no jealousy concerning his powers. Our heads were close over manuscripts by candlelight until the morning star appeared and we stretched our backs before having a short and deep sleep in a still embrace beneath the skins.

One night I asked if he did not want to have me as his wife. This I whispered into his ear as we lay together in darkness so thick that we could not see each other. He finally asked if I wanted to be his wife, and I told him the truth—that that desire had become larger than any other. I tasted the skin of his shoulders and lightly bit his neck. Instead of turning to me with passion, he made noises of agitation, as though an insect had gotten beneath his clothing. He moved away from me, and a sorrow that I have never known before or since spread through me like blood dropped into a cup of water. I could not move and believed that Giannon the druid had performed a spell that was killing me. I spent that night in the darkness outside, cold to the core of my body.

After this night of dark aloneness, I went into the woods many times to perform rituals with the aim of getting help from the fertile powers of nature in waking Giannon's lust. These were days of great restlessness, and I well understood Eve's determination to awaken some desire in Adam, even if it be desire for forbidden fruit. After I had been with Giannon for four months, I told him that I wanted his child, and then he parted my legs and made me his wife. On this night I believed that his soul had entered mine and created an intimacy with roots so deep that I would never be cold or thirsty or hungry again. I was unable to tell the difference between his pleasure and mine. And when we rested, I wanted to stay always beside him and say more things than we had said, revealing more and probing our histories and ambitions together for many different lifetimes. I believed then in the transmigration of souls, and I vowed to live every incarnation beside Giannon. But he rose quickly from the bed, compelled to tend and nurture his garden as soon as there was light enough to distinguish one blade of grass from another. It conjures sadness in me even now to remember those days, for I had hopes that were never made solid but which always seemed sweet.

Giannon often traveled, and the distance between us was filled with private efforts, his tending to the news and needs of many *túath*s and my studying the scrolls. Sometimes there were visitors who came, men and women of mysterious intent. When they saw me there instead of Giannon, they stayed and let their eyes wander over all the items in the dwelling. When Giannon received them, they whispered to each other and parted solemnly. Giannon did not like conversation and gave only small morsels of information about his adventures away from our home. When I asked to accompany him, he told me that I had to wait until I knew the primary stories and could present myself as an advanced apprentice. Soon I deduced that Giannon had some encounters with Christian clergy. Of these matters he was particularly secretive, but he learned Latin and brought seed to his garden which he called by their Latin names.

I did not swell, and Giannon grew agitated at the futile effort to place a child in my womb. He did praise my intelligence, and he also came to me with joyful eagerness when his work in the garden produced thriving new plants. Let me say here that I was never mistreated by Giannon, and only once do I remember a blow from his hand. It came one night when I asked him for that which he did not want to give. Anger is the sin that plagues me most, and I am loathe to be shamed for my desires. When Giannon mimicked me with clever imitation of a woman's whine, I tried to strike him. He felt only the breeze of my hand as it passed his face, and in quick response he struck the side of my face. In the dark we were silent, both of us ashamed.

I never had any doubt of Giannon's respect for me, though our methods of working were not the same. I brought passion and impulse to all that I learned, or I did not learn well. He had discipline and a careful pace. After we had been together for two years, he asked me to help him transcribe laws and histories on the scrolls. He also listened with respect to my intuitions about the spirits of wild plants and animals. But he wearied quickly of conversation involving my fears and complaints. He became angry sometimes when I lay beside him or touched his face; he winced as though he were being preyed upon by an unsavory and inept predator. When he shunned me, I felt my mother's wild spirit in me and raged like a caged bear. I learned to like solitude when he loved it; but I never wandered far from a sorrow that grew in place of the child we never had. May God forgive me for my self-pity.

There was one night when a storm raged between us and he said that he was not like other men. He did not have lust for women as other men did. He said powerful words, as destructive as his satires. They entered me like spirit blades because I loved the mouth from which the words came and the tongue that moved to say them. I loved the eyes and knew the soul behind them. I loved the hands that could make people and histories and beauty appear on a piece of parchment. I became full of shame that my body was too small or my features too plain to arouse him. I wished that my hair was the color of raven feathers, shining blue when sunlight flowed over it, instead of the color of rust on an old warrior's sword. I wished that I had the grace and discipline of a chieftain's daughter who rode tall horses and could not want a man as a husband before ten wanted her. I wished that I were as compelling as Mebd of Connacht, who cohabited with nine kings, who all loved her well. Then Giannon would untether his passion and grace me with it. At that time, I did not know that the love of God is greater than the love of humans, though still I wonder if humans are not the vessels from which we drink God's love. But then I am an ignorant pagan, only late in my life surrendered to the new religion. And still I say, because I am weak and blasphemous, that if Giannon had given me full affection before we were roughly parted, and if I had lost my shame, perhaps I would not have lain on the threshold of the Chapel of Saint Brigit and asked to be embraced by the Christian Church, allowed to share its worldly knowledge. Must we suffer, as the Greeks have said, in order to be led to a greater wisdom than the one we would have settled for?

Giannon himself encouraged me to accept the Christians and listen to their lessons. He knew well how sacred words and knowledge were to me, and he admitted that the monks knew many languages, that there were many words and lands and methods and stories in the world that the monks studied and recorded, more than any druid knew. One noon when he had been gone for many months to bury a chieftain's daughter in a *túath* to the west, he returned with a companion. I heard men's laughter when I was bent over a tablet, writing from memory the story of the prophetess Scathach, who trained Cuchulain to be a hero. While thinking upon her technique of severing an enemy's arm from his body, I was startled and frightened to hear men's laughter, for Giannon did not often make sounds of merriment, and he rarely welcomed company. I came out of the dwelling to see him walking up the hill to our home beside a man who had his hand on Giannon's shoulder. The two of them conversed and laughed. What made my brow gather in wonderment was that the man with him was tonsured. He was a Christian monk with merry eyes and a frame almost as small as mine, named Mongan.

I nodded a greeting, being struck mute, and prepared some porridge. Giannon had brought the ale that was given to him as payment for his part in the burial. We three sat outside, the monk and Giannon discussing the plants in the garden. The monk was young, hardly a man, but full of knowledge and skill. He had with him an *editorulgatu*.* He taught me about the conversion of Brigit by Saint Patrick and told me of some of her miracles, including the conversion of water into ale. I opened my palm to him and challenged him, saying that his kind made soot out of soil and harassed the druids. I asked if his kind did not lose their senses when they cut their hair, and he asked if I did not worry that the pork I ate had been some druid in trans-

---

*Editorulgatu: common Latin version of the Bible, based on a translation by Saint Jerome.

mutation. We made many jokes that are now dangerous, for in those times there was not so much fear of contradiction, but a love of discourse. Our talk was passionate and friendly, and we drank to Brigit until I was howling like a wolf beneath a half moon. Giannon said that I was a *bean sidhe.** I do not remember clearly any other events of that night, except that Giannon did not lie beside me, and I had one *aisling*† after another. Between visions of flaming candles falling into deep crevasses and rings of stone sinking into the ground, I heard the laughter of the two men. I also dreamed that Mebd brought me the severed arm of a man, and when I held his hand and kissed it, he became whole and his eyes were those of my mother.

---

*Bean sidhe: woman of the fairies.
†*Aisling:* mystical vision or dream.

SEVENTH INTERRUPTION

THESE DAYS ARE FULL of foul mysteries and dim intentions. The infant's grave was defiled again. This time, the stones seem to have burst from their pile. They were strewn about, some as far away as twenty paces, and the cross was thrust upside down in the center of the mound. Sister Luirrenn and I stood as though turned to stone beside the little grave, and she asked if I had heard any violent noises while I watched over Brigit's flame. I told her that the wind had been strong and made the shutters knock against the walls. The persistent perversion has created a silence and fear among us all. And there has been an accident among the laypeople who live around the convent, adding to the dread. A man's foot was crushed and torn from him by a wild pig he had wounded. He was brought back to his home by his brothers, one of whom had himself lost three fingers in a boar hunt two years before. We are all praying for the man's recovery, and more for his soul, as recovery is not likely. I have seen his face, and its pale trembling I have seen in other faces when death was near. Death grins at us and defies our faith and hope. The woman whose infant died and whose grave has been defiled is my shadow when I go among the lay dwellings. She whispers to me. She tells me that she knew the danger of looking into her infant's eyes and seeing its soul as a part of her own. Now she says that she is not whole, but a ghost herself. I hold her firmly and say that I feel her solid form and warm flesh, and that I will pray for her child's soul. She says that she does not want my prayers, and she spits on my cloak. But then she kneels and kisses my feet. She asks while sobbing, is it better to think that the infant, whose smile was broad and wise before it took sick, has gone to heaven, or that he has become another child somewhere, smiling into the face of another woman? She asks, if the child goes to the Christian heaven, will he remain an infant, or grow to be a man whom she will not know if she goes to heaven as well? The abbot calls her questions madness. I see their wisdom and grasp her hands, which are stained with the same black dirt that is beneath her ragged nails. I told her to hide her hands from the other sisters and the abbot, who calls women witches when they do not please him.

The abbot spoke at the noonday recital of psalms, saying again that demons are among us. He told us that these demons thirst for blood and have faces so twisted that one would die of terror if one looked upon them. He also said that these demons come up through the ground and wrap their long hands around the ankles of the weak in spirit, dragging them down to hell to be transformed into servants of their ruinous ambitions. And sometimes these demons wear masks and walk about at night, pretending to be familiar persons. He addressed the nuns particularly, saying that women are the natural allies of demons. He warned us to keep no company with the women who go into the woods and gather herbs and to tell them that their actions are evil. He called these women witches and said that we should not suffer one to live, nor should we suffer astrologers to live, for astrologers are like demons who can transform themselves into bestial forms. I am thinking of my mother and her pure and wise knowledge of the deep woods. I am remembering a time when she threw back her head and howled when a pack of wolves drank from the other side of the lake. She laughed when they raised their dripping muzzles and stared at her. Would this abbot praise her death and call the worms that consumed her the agents of God's will? I cannot consider this matter long or I will pull my hair from my head. I have, though, begged the abbot to cease telling the woman whose infant died that demons have taken her child to hell because it was not protected by Christian ritual and faith. This increases the poor woman's mad sorrow.

After the abbot's sermon, the other sisters and I walked solemnly into the cold, damp air and felt oppressed. We did not consult one another on the content of the lesson and ate little at the afternoon meal. Sister Aillenn called to me to come to the high place where she stood so I could watch beside her. The two wild horses that no one has been able to catch were in the cleared valley below. They ran with arched tails, and I saw that they calmed and pleased Sister Aillenn, who said without looking at me, "I had once a horse as powerful as that." And then she recognized me and told me that those two horses had been warriors' beasts, used in many battles. And then their masters were killed and none other could take them as they ran from the battle and freed themselves. And so they have become wild, refusing any human master. I have heard this same story told of the horses by the people in the settlement who have tried to harness them. I did not tell Sister Aillenn that these beasts had trampled a man, whose body I had then wrapped in blankets so that his broken bones were kept still as he died.

And now I can hear Sister Aillenn as though renewed in her private and tormented rituals. I will soon put wax in my ears, for I cannot stand to hear her moans and unearthly cries. I am afraid that we will all go mad. I can guess that the abbot as confessor asked her, as he asked me, if she had anything to say concerning the molesting of the grave. I felt cold in my stomach to think that there was any suspicion of me in this matter. The man was stern but did not press his inquiry when I rose to leave. I suggested then that he allow the unbaptized to be buried in the sanctioned cemetery. He did not reply. I am afraid that my folios will be found and read, and I will be cast out for not dedicating all my talents and materials to Christian or scholarly transcription. This abbot inspires fear. He has seeped into a position of influence like one who steals a single crumb at a time until the whole cake is gone. And we ask each other, one sister to another, how it has happened that this man has come to abide with us as a brother and now behaves like a chieftain when we did not endow him with such privilege.

I have said that we should consider a gentle request that he leave our convent to build his own monastery in another place. I dared not speak this in front of Sister Luirrenn, but only to a gathering of five sisters who worked in the garden. Sister Aillenn was one of them, and after I spoke she came to me and struck me hard across my face. "You are a demon, little Gwynneve," she said. And the other sisters looked away.

[8]

LET IT BE KNOWN HERE that Giannon was a good man, unacquainted with demons. But he had dark moods, which caused him to be ungentle. After we had lived together for several years, he was less often summoned to the homes of chieftains, because they had come to fear his sharp satires. They wanted the powerful magic of other druids, who performed with smoke and crystals. In those times, many druids sought to hold their power with tricks that Giannon disdained. They manipulated fire and claimed to metamorphose into beasts and birds. Some druids encouraged one chieftain to attack another, thereby enlarging the influence of the dominant chieftain and his attending druid as well. No longer were druids free to roam from one allegiance to another, free of threat, for they were all threatened now by the tonsured men and needed protection from pagan chieftains. There was violence between druids and Christian priests, and between Christian and Christian. And it happened that the *oblaire* with the forked beard had his head held beneath the waters of a lake until he drowned. This happened in a *túath* in which the chieftain had been converted to the Christianity of pope and priest.

When I had been with Giannon for seven years and had learned almost three hundred stories but borne no child, the gleemen who had been my companions visited our home. They were no longer five but four. Solemnly the woman told me that the *oblaire* had thought the Christians of a lake *túath* were his brothers, but the priest who attended the chieftain told the people of that *túath* that the *oblaire*'s beliefs were demonic heresy. The woman stood knocking her head against the herbs hanging in our dwelling to show how the *oblaire* had preached that Christians did not need the intervention of clergy in their communion with God. He had opened a cage and let free the ravens inside as a demonstration of the freedom of a man's soul to soar to God's heaven on its own wings. The trumpeter's antics did not dilute the *oblaire*'s insult to the priests. During the night, when the troupe was camped outside the wall that ringed the *túath,* some men came to them and took the *oblaire* away to the lake and drowned him. The lesser juggler, who had been my husband, assaulted the men with a large branch and killed one of them. The troupe fled and came to Giannon's home, knowing I lived there and hoping to make plans without being molested by those who wanted revenge.

We sat in silence, except for my weeping at the news, which was a new wound for me and sore with fondness for the old gleeman. I could not see what help there was in our small clearing. Giannon brought out ale, and we considered the methods by which a man can hide himself in this land. We discussed other matters, and I hid my face with my hair when the woman began to tell of the times when I stole bread and whole cabbages from the *túaths* our company visited. She said, "She went in the night as a maiden, and came back the same night full grown with child." She put out her hand to show the hill made of foodstuffs that I had carried under my clothing. I was glad they could be merry, but they brought trouble into our home. Giannon became angry when the half-wit wandered into the garden and trampled some of the herbs there. His temper silenced us, and when the lesser juggler touched my hand and looked into my eyes, I rose and said that we had little to offer but would help them fill their packs with goods for their journey. I never saw those gleemen again and think often of them disappearing down the hill, the five become four, and the half-wit slouching like a beast. Giannon stood straight as a tree with his curling tendrils dancing in a breeze like ribbons, watching the troupe disappear. And he said to me with firm wisdom, "Everything is changing." And I felt that we two knew the secrets of these changes, the sadness and danger, and we two had a vision together of a world constantly transforming through countless births and deaths, its noises becoming deafening and cruel.

I stayed there with Giannon, and in all those years I was hungry for his affection and wanted it far more than it was given. I think now that I was a child still yearning for her mother. But a husband's hands on his wife can be soothing, and I admired Giannon's hands for their slow and careful attention to any task. I was more apprentice than wife. As proof of our kinship, Giannon and I erected an *ogham* a mile into the woods to the northwest of our clearing. I cannot say what we wrote on this stone. It cannot be spoken or written elsewhere. But it marked the time when I had spent nine years as his apprentice. In those nine years I had learned all that he knew about making and reading marks. But I did not have his child and reconciled myself to being barren. It was another sign that I was to be a druid and serve the people of this land, immortalizing their lives and their laws rather than my own lineage. It was tedious to learn the laws and their variations from *túath* to *túath*. I still know the value of a hostage according to the person's age, birth, gender, and talents. I still know the way to list a woman's property and separate it from her husband's. I can still tell the configurations of the stars and have learned also the Greek names for them. I am aware, too, of the influence of seasons and the length of days. The three hundred and fifty stories are confused in my mind now, one bull in one story confused with a pig in another, many heroes seeming like one. I fear that all these stories will be lost or changed until everything will have been somehow achieved by Saint Patrick, though the deeds were first spoken of twenty lifetimes before his.

In our lessons I achieved an intimacy with Giannon I have known with no other man or woman, and this intimacy finally overwhelmed my need for my mother. In learning the configurations of the stars in all seasons, I lay with my back on Giannon's chest, my head next to his, resting on his shoulder, as both of us looked up at the wanderers and fixed suns revealed in the night sky. He held my hand with his and pointed them both at the stars as he gave their names and influences. We bathed together in the stream nearby, we ate together, and though Giannon despised words that had no importance, the silences we shared were full of understanding. I clung to Giannon in the night and was kept warm by him. We were twin souls, forgiven one by the other for the disappointments and terrible words of those many years when I fought too hard to extract from him the affection I wanted. In our years together, we had faced illness and fear together, as well as the concerns of all creatures for simple food and shelter. I began to accept the limitations of my life and the alteration of my aspirations, an acceptance that younger women consider weakness and surrender. But I found that the limitations I accepted, as youth and its dreams fell away, composed a narrow and secret passage leading to an expanse of space and liberation I had not realized existed. I began to prefer peaceful surrender to noble battle, for in peace is an internal freedom one never has in war, though sometimes warring is necessary for external freedom. The disappointments were not bitter, because I was with a companion who did not turn his back on truth.

Among all the wisdom and facts I learned from Giannon, I also learned the loneliness of incarnation, in which there is inevitably a separation of souls because of the uniqueness of our faces and our experiences. And I learned also the moments when the current of my life joins the current of another life, and I can glimpse for a moment the one flowing body of water we all compose. We sat sometimes in silence and apart on clear nights, making notes on the stars and the occurrence of comets, which came more frequently in those days, as though the gods were throwing fire at each other in the heavens in a battle for our souls. We did not have to speak to know that we each wondered to what purpose we existed and to what end our efforts took us. For we both were weak in doctrine and strong in questions. But we both loved effort and knowledge, though I saw Giannon become weary in his eyes.

I do not understand a man who does not want to know all that he can know. Why would anyone choose ignorance? If he chooses ignorance because he is lazy, then he is a fool, for the ignorant are put to hard labor digging and hauling stones for masters who tell them they need no knowledge. If a man must labor from dawn to dusk to avoid a blow on the head and to earn a cup of grain, he has no time to gain knowledge and remains a slave to masters. I think, therefore, that it is a worthy vocation to free a man enough that he can learn who he is and what he is capable of, where he came from and what philosophies steer his life. Teaching is a sacred art. This is why the noblest druid is not the one who conjures fires and smoke but the one who brings the news and passes on the histories. The teacher, the bard, the singer of tales is a freer of men's minds and bodies, especially when he roams without allegiance to one chieftain or another. But he is also a danger to the masters if he insists upon telling the truth. The truth will inevitably cause tremors in those who cling to power without honoring justice.

In the summer before Giannon's disappearance, we determined to compose together a satire. It was to concern the chieftain in whose *túath* the *oblaire* had been drowned. Giannon knew that this crime agitated me, and he enjoyed his satires, for they took advantage of his sharp wit and thorny spirit. He had scrolls concerning the feats of this chieftain before his conversion, and we conspired to use them to show his fickle claims. We knew the danger of this effort and told ourselves we would bury the document beneath the stone in the woods for the earth to consume and disseminate as vapor through the land. In this way the chieftain's demise would be slow and hard to attribute. We gave insulting names to the tonsured men and the priest who had converted the *túath,* and in our words we turned the people of the *túath* into rodents and pigs. When we were done and I prepared to take the scroll to the woods for burial, Giannon would not let me, saying he had not finished. For three days, he did not sleep or work in his garden but stayed by sunlight and rush light at the table.

I saw what he wrote, and I did not understand its purpose. He had turned to a satire of the druids, naming particular men and women, some of whom had great powers. He made their limbs wither and ridiculed their transformations into wind and lark. He recalled prophecies they had made that had not been fulfilled. This frightened me greatly, and I begged him to burn the words and swallow the smoke. This was one of the nights that made me old. Giannon, my twin soul, said that he would tell a satire of my own life. His words were witty and cruel. He said I still suckled my mother and had the body of a girl. He said that I had weeds growing in my womb. I knew that he could kill me with his words, and I went into the woods and slept the night against the stone. We did not speak of the scroll in the following days. But he told me that he had not meant to fling painful words at me and that he was, in truth, haunted by the vision of the *oblaire*'s head held beneath the water, his forked beard floating like lake rushes beside him when his struggle ended. He said, "I am weary to sickness of men who do not till the soil or feed the pigs and who make those who do say certain words or die, whether they be druids' words or priests' words." Giannon traveled then, and I later learned that he went to that *túath* and read the satire. I do not know what harm it did, but it was connected with the visitors who came to speak with us in the spring of that year.

One winter evening in the tenth year that I was with Giannon, three druids came to see us, their forms black and foreboding against the pale evening sky. They seemed to be the darkness itself, in human form before it spread over the world and became night. We lit the rush lights and made a fire in the corner hearth. In this hut of warmth we five sat on mats and clothing , and we shared a sweet wine that the woman had brought. This woman I had seen before. She wore a large bronze circle on a tether around her neck. There were dark circles around her eyes that made them seem like empty shadows under the hood of her cloak. Her companions were a very old man composed of bones covered by a leathered skin, and a man with orange hair and beard that absorbed the energy and colors of our fire. When the woman lowered her hood, we saw that her hair had been shorn and her head rubbed with a pumice stone so that she was bald and her scalp red and cut. None of them had spoken until she showed her head and said, "I welcome your satires about the Christians, Giannon. This is what the Christians have done to me." I lowered my head, but Giannon looked full into her eyes and said, "What of it?" I wanted to strike him because of his surliness, which always stung me even when I was not its target.

The woman then explained her complaint, having established her right as a victim to complain. These are words that even devout Christians must hear. She said, "The new priests have divided the world into good and evil, separating things of the sky from things of the earth. They teach that the things of the earth are evil and all those who do not follow their laws are evil."

Giannon responded with impatience, rising and thrusting a stick into the fire. He said, "All I have asked is to be left alone so that I may grow plants in my garden and not have them trampled. Anyone who comes to me saying that he knows the truth is a liar or an idiot. I am weary to my marrow with various truths."

The old man could barely lift his head because his neck had hardened and left him always looking at the ground, but he used great effort to move and see Giannon. Trembling with that effort, he said, "You wish to be killed, Giannon? They are killing druids, those whom you include in your satires. Whom do you spare from your destructive wit?"

Giannon was bitter even with this weak old man and said, "I am through with stories of religious magic and political crimes. These stories are used to make people afraid and easily told what to do." I traded glances with the orange-haired man and wondered if he would speak. Silence followed as we all looked at the fire. I thought of the gleemen and the monks clearing the land with their big fires. I thought of the monk Giannon had brought home one night. And then Giannon said, "They have made improvements. I have new plants that grow when there is frost. There are better plows and new languages and histories."

The woman grabbed the leather strip from which the bronze circle hung and held it in her fist as though she were holding herself back like a horse that might run wild. She said, "They will suffer for it. For each improvement there is a huge cost, as huge as the heavens, as huge as the souls of every person on the earth."

Giannon said to her, "You speak like a man reciting a heroic legend."

The man with the red beard stood up and came near to Giannon so that they shared each other's breath. He said, "When did you become our enemy?"

I did not want to see them wrestle, so I stood up and came between them. I said, "He is not a Christian. Look—there is no cross here." I was afraid.

The man spoke again, standing above me so that, though I was between him and Giannon, he could lean forward and touch Giannon's nose with his own. He said, "If you are not a Christian, then remember that you are a druid. We are gathering, all of us, to make a plan, to use our rituals to renew our powers."

Giannon did not answer but sat again. The woman asked me, "You are druid now. What do you say?" I looked to the floor and did not speak.

Then the woman began to weep and came to the orange-bearded man and pounded on his chest. She wailed, leaning back so that the hood fell off and showed in the firelight her bare and welted head. The man could not stop her fit, and she began to scream, "We are lost! We are lost!" And I was chilled with cold bumps on my skin, though Giannon stared into the fire, musing quietly to himself. The old man's head shook and his eyes were wide as he stared helplessly at the legs of the table.

Finally the woman quieted and helped the old man to his feet. Slowly they left the dwelling. The bearded man, who was left behind, threw something into the air that looked like dust and all the flames went out, the fire as well as the rush lights. In the darkness I stood as still as a rabbit cornered by a fox, and then I heard Giannon say, "These are tricks for some fair."

I knew then, in sorrow and loneliness, that Giannon's bitterness had become greater than his desire for truth. He had been defeated and our souls separated, though I never understood by what.

EIGHTH INTERRUPTION

THERE IS NEWS. There has been mild weather, though it is time for winter. The ground is still soft, the frost having penetrated only a little. In such weather, the sisters still tend the garden, hoping to nurture the last cabbages and have them fresh for our meals. And so early this morning, I was laying dried grasses around them to keep them warm in the early morning. The sun had come out and lifted fog from the ground that mingled with my own white breath. I was shivering with cold and stood to stretch my back. A wind blew the fog so that I could see the infant's grave, and I was afraid of what I saw. For again there was desecration and chaos where the stones had been neatly piled. I walked to where the ruins were and saw that this time there was a hole filled with white fog where the grave had been. I squatted there and breathed into the hole so that the fog floated out. There was no corpse. The infant, which by now must be ruined by worms and dampness, is gone.

When I rose, Sister Luirrenn was behind me, wringing her hands. I looked toward the lay houses, down the hill. We stood without speaking until she went down on her knees and pulled me beside her, where we prayed, moving our lips against our joined hands. What terror is this? What force of sorrow or evil takes the dead from their graves? I would rather believe that the infant's soul has formed a new life in a new body, though I know this is heresy. But I would rather believe this, dear Brigit who protects mothers and their babes, than that the tiny boy is tormented in Limbo, feeling its decayed body as an unspeakable pain still tethering it to the terror and pain of its mother. Were its body a thing like a cloak, discarded when it was worn and useless, my horror would be less. I know the stench of a corpse, and it is not the sweet smell of an infant's skin. Whoever holds a corpse to her aching breasts will go mad. Whatever defiles a corpse is already mad.

This event has been the unfortunate greeting for a new monk who has been whispered about throughout the convent. For he does not speak even to say the psalms. He has been damaged in some way but works hard making a new garden. He is one of the Christians Giannon used to praise for his knowledge of new seeds and methods. He is an old man but has a straight back. His face is full of a wild gray beard, whereas he has no hair on his head, so he wears a large straw hat as I have seen worn in the south to keep sun and rain from molesting his scalp. He is an odd soul, but he comforts us with his labor and has increased our crops and therefore decreased our hunger. I watched the hard concentration with which he began his task in a patch of earth occupied by stubborn and lazy rocks, stones that have made deep nests for themselves. I wondered at first if this new man had a hand in exhuming the infant, as though it made the ground unclean. I wanted to blame him rather than accuse any we have known and lived with for so long here. But he is innocent, for he was on his knees throughout the night by the abbot's bedside in order to indicate, without words, his strong desire to join the monks. There is a rumor that his tongue was cut out by druids. But I do not believe this tale, for there is no reason for such cruelty and many rumors about druids are lies.

I wonder that this place brings to it so many damaged and disturbed souls, such as Sister Aillenn, whom I have two nights this fortnight found wandering naked and welted among the *clochan*s. And now there is this monk who cannot form words in his mouth. If there were not the law of celibacy for monks and nuns, I would encourage these two to become husband and wife and establish a clan of the strangely wounded. I wonder if we are a tribe of men and women searching for the truth, or a tribe of men and women hiding from the truth. When in our appeals to the unseen do we step from devotion to delusion? There are many times when I despise my doubts and desire complete faith in anything. I wish that Christ would touch me with his hand that is stained with blood and blistered from the wood of the cross that he carried to his own sacrifice. Or I wish that the sea god Manannan, whose breath is like cool mist, would kindly bring to me one of his magic pigs, which could be consumed and yet live again the next day. I hunger for both the meat and the comfort of miracles.

I have not yet heard what the abbot has said about the

matter of the infant's grave. I am afraid of him. I have doubts now that I belong here, for I avoid the abbot's authority and dread his intervention into the business of the nuns. But I love Brigit and need her protection. I pray that these words I am putting down on these parchments are not conjuring the chaos and evil that besets us. I am small and intend no harm. And sometimes weariness and hunger cause confusion and I wonder why no god, either old or new, gives us direct solace and understanding. The abbot says that only clerics receive direct messages from the new god, who tells him what is true and what is false. But he has a sour mouth and eyes that seem more full of fear than certainty. Perhaps I am not wise enough to understand the word of a god who was made flesh and then cruelly killed. I am simple, and I want, more than even food or Christ, to lie in the arms of Brigit and feel her long fingers stroke my hair as she sings of the lark and the yellow gorse.

[9]

THIS IS THE TIME to record the disappearance of Giannon the Druid, who deserved no punishment. I have told only the truth of his life as I knew it, and though he suffered others to endure his black moods and his satires, he did no evil and told no lies. He gave me knowledge and skills and as much affection as he had. I believe that much of his affection was stolen from him, in circumstances I do not know about, and replaced with bitterness. He should be regarded as similar to the druid who raised Brigit, and she, after all, used her druidic powers for Christian good. I have not seen Giannon for eleven years but still know his face and voice as though he lay beside me every night. He comes to me in dreams, though he does not speak. I see him standing or walking to me, and he kneels before me as though to receive a blessing from me. That is all.

After the visit from his druid cohorts, Giannon had no words about them. I scolded him once for clothing himself in thorns and letting no one near him. Then I returned to the peace I knew with the scrolls and my days in the woods.

The winter was hard, I remember, for we were hungry and cold. I asked the spirits of the woods to provide us with the cauldron of the Daghda, from which no one departs unsatisfied. And though the creatures of the forest, especially the wolf and even the fern frond, were full of kind and silent wisdom, none of them were transformed into great beings who could perform unnatural miracles. I went at that time into a *túath* as a druid. I told two stories for the chieftain as entertainment for a party of warriors who had taken seven cows from another *túath*. The feast was great, and I took more of the meat than was paid to me. When I walked home I saw a dead man, frozen and leaning against a tree, his cloak stiff and frosted. I should have seen that this was an omen.

When the ground began to soften and Giannon was occupied from dawn until sunset with his garden, I traveled more into other *túath*s. For Giannon grew blooms the color of birds' wings and grasses like plumes, but he scorned the growing of cabbages and grain. He had no interest in providing food for the stomach. I carried a pack of scrolls and herbs on my back that was almost as large as my own body. I knew some rituals and attended burials when there was no other priest to do so. I knew the *fled co-lige** and led the wailing and clapping of hands. I recited lamentations of sorrow. Never did I participate in the smashing of the death cart without thinking of my mother, and I hoped that the dead were comforted by our grief, though now I think it better to comfort them before they are dead. I stayed away

---

**Fled co-lige:* feast of the deathbed.

[116]

from the Christian *túaths*, having to alter my old notion that the *aes dána* could go past any walls. These separations seemed trivial to me, like rules in a game of hurling that are made to enhance the challenge. When I saw other druids, they did not speak to me or share with me secret plans and meetings. I knew that this was so because I lived with Giannon. Once a chieftain told me that Giannon could have been the most powerful druid in Ireland and that, even though he hid himself away, the power of his satires was feared more than disease or battle.

Giannon did not resent my vocation but resented the people who spoke of him as a dead man who had not been as great as they had thought him to be. He told me that performing tricks had become more important than telling the truth, because the druids, desperate to fight the tricks of the Christians, had become gleemen. I do not know which of his enemies came for Giannon, but I remember each detail of the night they came. I was lying with my hands on Giannon's chest, my legs woven with his. A terrible sound woke us, and I thought the walls of our dwelling were falling in a raging wind. Giannon sat up and threw the covers away from him and over me. He told me to be still and lie flat. I cannot forget his calm. There were four persons standing in our home, hooded in deep cowls and each holding a rush light. They held their fires out in front of them so as to blind us from seeing their faces. Without words, two pulled Giannon to his feet. I cried out, and he said for me to be quiet. Giannon asked them to allow him to dress warmly, as though he had expected them and knew that he was to go with them. He put on his leggings and tunic as I uncovered myself and pulled at his legs and hands. I said quietly, "Giannon, do not leave me." He said, with the impatience I had finally come to accept, "I am not leaving. I am being taken."

While he dressed, the hooded persons looked about, touching the scrolls and examining the herbs. And I asked Giannon, "Why are they taking you?" He answered, "I do not know, Gwynn. Be calm. It is best not to know. There will be no one to accuse, and I will return." Though I wore only a thin tunic, I left the bed and pleaded with the persons who stood like soulless things serving a power they would not name. I said, "Tell us what you want. We will give it. Tell us what we have done, and we will publicly renounce it." Two of the persons took Giannon out, and the others began to smash the jars and platters, spilling seed and oils. They gathered scrolls by the armful and threw them out. I clothed myself and went outside.

The two pigs we had were squealing in their pen, for a fire had been built near them into which one of the strangers threw scrolls and dried herbs. The smoke from this fire went straight up in a coiled pillar to the constellation of dogs. I spoke, hardly able to catch my breath, as though I had been running. I said, "If you are Christians, teach us. We are ignorant. We have no doctrine." But they moved like deaf spirits, now pulling up plants in Giannon's garden and flinging them into the fire. Then Giannon's legs weakened, and he whispered, "Brother, please." I went to him but was kicked away by one of the strangers. I called out, "I will go

with you. I will not be left behind. We will go together."
Giannon said no. He told me to go away from the dwelling,
that he would find me later.

The intruders then pulled Giannon up to stand and
pushed him forward. I ran behind and heard the pigs
scream as their fence was knocked down and they were
kicked into the woods, where, I was comforted to think, the
wolves would swiftly kill them and be sustained by them
even if Giannon and I were to starve. The hooded people
went to horses they had tethered to trees at the edge of the
woods, between our clearing and the *túath*. My fear of
horses seemed trivial, and I pulled at their manes and was
knocked to the ground many times when they reared and
screamed. One of the strangers was also knocked to the
ground when I frightened his horse. He lifted me up and
ran with me over his shoulder to the dwelling, where he
threw me on the fire, but I ran down the hill with flames on
my back to where Giannon and the others were on their
horses. I felt the heat on my skin and shed the cloak as the
horses galloped away. I stood watching them ride the edge
of the woods until it curved and I could not see them. Then
I felt the sting on my back where the fire had burned me.
I called out Giannon's name three times, but I heard nothing, not even an owl or wolf.

The fire they had made now smoldered, and I crouched
beside it, holding my legs. Cold air crawled on my bare
back. I shivered so hard that I could not stand up, so I lay
on the ground, shaking and biting my own tongue. I believed that I was dying and prayed to the earth to warm me

and comfort my soul. I wanted then, more than life, a companion to touch me as I died. When morning came and I was not dead, I crawled into the dwelling and lay down on the bedding. My back hurt so that I could not lie on it or even put cloth against it. I thought of every sign concerning Giannon's abduction. I thought of the anger of the druids whom he had insulted and dismissed. I thought of the stories of monks murdering druids. I thought of the rage of chieftains whom he had ruined with satire. And my mind would not be pulled back from the visions of his death at the hands of druids, who would, according to their rule, drown him, strangle him, and break his skull, all three; or at the hands of monks, who, it was said, would torment their captive with severe pain by means of cutting and burning until he converted and then was blessed and allowed to die; or by the hands of a chieftain, who would do the task forthrightly with sword or club. How horrible to wish for the chieftain's crude and honest method, whereas the other two pretend that their cruelty is for a noble and righteous purpose.

And now I think of the abbot. I can imagine a man such as he, who seems cold to suffering, throwing a small woman into a fire. He dislikes the strength of my stare when he declares who will go to Paradise and who will go to hell. The abbot would know that Giannon is in hell, whereas I know, since I am not fully converted or truly baptized, that Giannon lives in another incarnation, perhaps as a mother, for he needs to practice his embraces. But when I am wiser and believe in hell, I will pray to God to put me there with

Giannon, for if in heaven there are men like the abbot, that would be hell to me.

I will destroy these pages, for they are dangerous and blasphemous, may God forgive me. But now I will lie down, for I tremble too hard.

NINTH INTERRUPTION

THESE ARE COLD NIGHTS, though winter has passed and we are near the time of Beltane. This night the wind has blown freezing rain against the *clochan*s so they are coated with a sheen that reflects the stars. The weather mimics the bitter mood that is in our community. I have stayed silent, obedient to Sister Luirrenn, for she is greatly agitated by the abbot's sermons that insist that the evil omens and occurrences in past months are serious matters. There is doom in his voice. This agitation has also inflicted Sister Aillenn, whom I had to care for through the night. I found her again wandering naked in a veil of frost that the evening air had laid upon her beautiful shoulders like a bride's cloak. So she would not freeze to death, I took her into my *clochan* and was an audience to her ranting, which made my own skin colder. It seemed possible that the cold fog that curled around the *clochan*s had been made by her breath. We held each other for warmth as many do on cold nights, so that there are *clochan*s where two sleep and *clochan*s that are empty.

Sister Aillenn tells black stories, claiming that the dead infant has entered her body. With a knife she has drawn a simple picture of a child on her abdomen as though her skin were a stone on which one carves symbols. This infant lies in bloodstains and old marks of her self-inflicted bruises and scratches. Her body is a field of battle, and I was sick to see it. I bathed her with a damp cloth and cold water, and she did not flinch at the touch, so accustomed was she to discomfort. I rubbed oil upon her skin, the precious oil used to soothe the cracks on our feet. And I found the rosemary, which I had hidden, and put it on her wounds. I clothed her in tunic and cape, and she clung to me as though I were her mother. I combed her hair, so fine to touch when I separated the tangles with my fingers, and my touch brought stories from her mind to my ears.

One of her fearful tales concerns the monk who gardens and cannot speak. She says that he wanders outside her *clochan* and has made it clear with his eyes that the infant's corpse is now inside her. I did not respond or argue but prepared a salve with lard and rosemary to put on the tips of her fingers, which looked to have been scalded or rubbed raw by some repeated and frantic task. In wild fear she tells me that she still sees me go to the woods with the laywomen to gather plants and dig in the earth for roots. In truth, I have done this, for there are valuable energies in these plants, and though I sound like a Pelagian, I say that these plants were made by God and must therefore be useful. Sister Aillenn held my hand away with the lard mixture on my fingers, holding hard my wrist and spying the salve as though it could move by itself to her skin. She said, "Do I tell the abbot that you are a *bean sidhe*?" But seeing how pale my face was at this threat, which is dangerous, she laughed and embraced me, whirling me around the small cell, whispering and weeping.

I then told her that I had seen herself and the abbot one night, in the chapel when she was to attend to Brigit's flame. I had passed by and heard banging on the chapel door, as though someone were pounding his fist against the wood to be let out. I parted the shutters on one window enough to peer in, and saw by the light of Brigit's flame Sister Aillenn with her legs like a belt around the abbot's waist, her back against the door as his thrusts knocked her against the wood. In that light, I saw her face as a spirit's face, as though she were an angel of ecstasy. I felt Brigit's passion as her lips parted and her eyes looked inward to her pleasure. I looked away and leaned against the stones to recover my breath, for I felt the passion with her. But I heard soon after the abbot weeping, and I ran from there to my *clochan.* I told Aillenn that this is what I knew of her rituals with the abbot and that I have told no one.

She became quiet, and I believe she was calmed by my frankness. Her madness seemed to have evaporated like a thin puddle of rain in sunlight. Then she looked into my eyes, her own so white and clear, and begged me to pray with her. So we said, *"Nos auten in nomine Dei nostri ambulabimus."** This recitation comforted her more, so that she spoke with lucid terms, forgetting her strange mythologies. Her narrative explained how she had come to the

---

*"We however shall walk in the name of Our God."

convent of Saint Brigit to tend the flame. I held her close to me so she could speak softly if there were listeners outside leaning into the doorway to hear our conversation, and so we could be warm, for the fire had burned to embers and there was no dry wood.

As some have guessed, Sister Aillenn was born the daughter of a chieftain. He himself was the son of Dubtach Maccu Lugil, the pagan who rose to honor Saint Patrick and so was blessed. In his and his heirs' *túath,* all but one became Christians, being visited often by the Britons, who were already converted. The one who remained a pagan was the chieftain's daughter Aillenn, who had always been timid of people and gatherings of any kind. This, she told me, was because she had fallen from a horse and damaged her ear and was confused by noise and attention until she learned to ignore those who spoke to her or to watch their mouths to see what words they formed. As she grew toward *aimsir-togu,* there were songs sung about her beauty and also about her skills with horses, which she loved more than human or god. She sang one of those songs for me, in which it was said that her eyes were haunted gems and she smelled of horses and slept with arrows. To these things she devoted herself. Her father urged her to be baptized and become a Christian, but she wanted only to groom and ride her horse, a black mare who was her companion from dawn to sunset. In desperation and for the salvation of his daughter's soul, the chieftain killed the mare. With horrible emotion, Sister Aillenn told me of the method of his cruelty: he pounded the horse's skull with a club as his daughter watched, held fast to a chair with cords. She saw its legs fold and collapse. Its face, which she had stroked and held against her own cheek, became an unrecognizable heap of ruin.

Aillenn grieved heavily, weeping day and night, unable to attend feast or games. She seemed more like a hostage or bonded woman than a chieftain's daughter. She did not comb her hair or brush her cloak. She wore a braid of her dead mare's hair around her neck, even when her father said that she had made a beast into a god and would be punished. He attached a great dowry to her as inducement to suitors to take her away, out of his sight. But all were afraid of her, and she hid her face with her hair when men approached her. Then a priest came to the *túath* to discipline the monks and sharpen their doctrine. He found Aillenn living in a corner of her father's home, sooted and despairing. She liked his eyes, which were brown like her mare's, and he came close to her and spoke into her ear so she was not confused. He spoke gently and told her stories of the saints, including Patrick and Brigit. He enticed her to eat by feeding her with his own hands and letting her suck upon his fingers.

She told me that they spoke to each other without words, and I knew well what she meant. I could have traded my own thoughts of Giannon for hers about this priest. They breathed like winded horses when they looked into each other's eyes, and they trembled if their fingers touched. With great tenderness the priest attached devices to her soft and flawless body in order to keep them both chaste. Aillenn showed me how the priest went down on his knees to put iron around her loins, his face so close to where he held a key that was like an iron flower. And they both loved the feel of the key, inserted into the lock and turned, barring her genitals from any penetration. The sound it made was more intimate than any other sound, and their passion for it was great. They consulted the chieftain's smith and had the black-stained man create pretty new devices in which to encase Aillenn's lean pelvis. The smith decorated the iron with Latin words and Christian symbols, which the priest touched with his lips. When Aillenn woke in the night from a vision of her horse's head crushed to pulp, the priest was beside her and distracted her from the pain of her thoughts and the pain of her loins with his philosophies. He told her that the mare was in heaven, its head restored. He moved her legs apart so the iron would not chafe her. He put salves upon the abrasions the metal made and washed the wounds that festered. He could not have enough of Aillenn, and she could not have enough of him. She washed his feet and tore his meat with her own teeth. She lifted the wine cup to his lips. Despite these diversions, the priest's agitation grew. Aillenn suffered fevers from the fetid wounds and humid enclosure of the iron. The priest looked for comfort in the scholarship of saints and found Saint Augustine to be a twin soul. Shadowed constantly by Aillenn, who says that she could not stop her desire, he began to be ill, unable to swallow his food. He had an epiphany, which told him that he had made a woman into an object of worship, having been seduced, like Adam, by lust and beauty. He prayed to be given the strength of Saint Au-

gustine, who had renounced his own mistress and acknowl-
edged original sin, which was a constant weakness that a
man had to battle in himself. The priest had fevers and
thought that he was going to die of the heat he and Aillenn
shared. He saw this heat as a foretelling of the hell they
would endure for eternity. He told Aillenn, with the wildness of fever, that the world was a horrible place in which
human flesh created hideous suffering. He muttered about
his mother being raped, about the promises, at least, of
heaven, of a place of beauty beyond the world of worms.
He asked, grasping her arm, which she mimicked by grasping my arm so that I thought it would be broken, "How can
we not believe and follow the Son of God, who promises
some purpose to this suffering and some laws to guide us
out of human agony and sorrow?"

And I was considering the notion that words cannot, after
all, lead us out of misery and the certainty of death. I was
also studying in my mind the matter of men who are afraid
of passion and of a woman's power to incite it. But I did not
speak, and instead listened on to Aillenn's tale.

When the priest was well, he spurned Aillenn, having
made a promise to God to do so were he to live. Is it not
strange to think of a man so intent upon heaven who yet
makes desperate promises to be spared passage to it? Poor
Aillenn crawled on her knees and held on to the hem of his
robes. Her penance was extreme, and she howled like a dying dog when the priest was sent to Kildare to be abbot to
the monks, who had begun to seek the protection of Brigit.
He joined the men who are brothers to the nuns to become

abbot and confessor and is the very man who came only a few seasons ago to our community and now gives sermons about our fetid souls. In his absence, Aillenn's state became so feeble that her father locked her in the stables and gave speeches to her, for as many hours as he had no duties, about the necessity of her not agitating the abbot or any other Christian cleric. He told his daughter with passionate effort that the only solace in the world of humans was power, and that the power now was with the Christians and their allies, and he saw no end to that power. He struck her to the ground and, standing over her, told her that she should betray all else and befriend the Christians in order to secure for their lineage the power that would soon rule this land and all others. She must prove herself not to be a fairy demon with her beauty and her seduction of holy men. She must do penance and represent her father and their family as a saint and nothing less. That, he said, is what she must become, for she would enrage the abbot if she were to marry. She must be a saint. He was sorely afraid of being less than chieftain and being remembered for a mad daughter who tormented an abbot's God-directed celibacy.

One day, Aillenn asked one of the bonded women to help her bathe and comb her hair. She let herself be fed and oiled, and then she walked into the *túath* and past rounded eyes and onto the road that led to Kildare, where the priest had gone. She had to travel many days without food or companionship until she came to the convent of Saint Brigit and lay herself on the threshold to be taken in.

I recall the change in the mood of the abbot and understand now that his agitation began when Aillenn came to us. Sister Aillenn told me that he filled up with anger when he saw her, and he forced a promise from her never to refer to the days when they had been together in her *túath*. He allowed her to stay only if she made this promise and stayed away from him. He scolded her for bringing herself to him to tempt and ruin his soul. He said that she suffocated him as though she lay her body across his face. He said also that, as long as her face and body were beautiful, he would not look at her, he would not say her name. He told her that his regard for her would be based solely on the devotion she gave to Christ and his saints. But then he came to her when she was guarding the flame in the chapel, and they did not speak except with their bodies, and then he wept and left her.

At the end of her account, Sister Aillenn wailed like a child and said that she had tried to be devoted and pure but that she attracts demons and is beset by them. She claimed again that a demon has entered the infant's corpse and come into her womb. She believes that the monk who does not speak is also a demon who watches her. She separated from me then and struck me hard across the face, and she said that I had seduced the story from her and was a demon myself. At this second time of being struck by this sister, I was heartsore to be so cruelly treated and sick with sudden loneliness. She made her eyes into narrow windows through which arrows are shot, and she said to me that indeed power was all that mollified misery. She said that she would align herself with whatever showed the greatest power as her father had taught her to do. She said that her father was a great chieftain who killed the mare because he was not weakened by affection of any kind. And I asked her if affection was not also a strong means of enduring human life. I said that men fear affection because it is stronger than power and one must only have brute force to wield power but must have strength deeper than flesh to wield affection. For with affection comes great sorrow, the sorrow of inevitable death, but also with affection comes joy and peace that power can never give. Aillenn asked me what good my affection had ever done, for I was barren and alone. This made me weep as she looked on, her chin raised as though she knew herself to be a chieftain's daughter. And here I say that a woman can ally herself with men's power as long as she has her youth to offer. But when a woman loses her youth, she will regret playing that game. And she will wish that she had learned instead the art of druid or warrior to make those less wise respect her capacity for affection. May God receive such arts as a holy offering, not meant as heresy. This I say with love for Saint Brigit and for the Mother of God, Mary, who was strong enough to be impregnated by the Holy Spirit and wise enough to raise Jesus Christ.

I fell asleep with supplications to God on my lips and woke too late to attend the morning psalms, ripped from sleep by an approaching thunder that rattled the stones of the *clochan* before fading away. I fled outside, fearing that the stones would come down on me. The sun was not yet above the horizon, and I saw in the early light the two wild horses, the brown mare and the gray stallion. They were galloping with arched tails down the hillside and along the edges of the valley below. In the middle of the open space, as though to defy the convent and flaunt their freedom, they mated. I did not look away and saw that a few yards away from me, in front of her own *clochan*, Sister Aillenn stood watching as well.

[10]

AFTER THE DISAPPEARANCE of Giannon, I stayed a fortnight in the dwelling, eating little and afraid to let my eyes close at night. I watched the hillside and the edge of the woods and thought many times that I saw a figure and that the figure I saw was Giannon returning. Every shadow and movement teased me until I believed that Bebo's fairies were using me for their entertainment. I went to the stone in the woods and made offerings of scrolls, feathers, herbs, and polished pebbles. At certain times of the day, when the words on the stone that Giannon and I had put there were illuminated by the sun, I stood before it and chanted whatever came to my head in praise of powers I knew and in supplication to them. These were pagan acts, which I did not know to be sins. May God and Saint Brigit understand the fear and soreness I felt. I begged to dream of Giannon and be told where he had gone and what happened to him. But all I dreamed of were the great fires that the tonsured men set, and these fires blew all over the land and blackened the ground and made the lakes boil.

My mind could not be still, and I thought of all the places where Giannon might have been taken. I wished to go myself to Teách Duinn* to search for him. Instead, I waited until the Fair of Tailltenn, where my mother had taken me when she went to the council of women. I took Giannon's own pack, filled it with his scrolls, and went west to meet the road to the fair. I looked well into every face I passed on the road and stopped at the public place to hear the voices there. They were all strangers that I heard and saw, not even one child or man from the *túath* of Tarbfhlaith. I felt strongly my loneliness on this earth and sometimes imagined that I was despised by the gods. I had no mother and no companion; I had not even a friend.

The Fair of Tailltenn that year did not thrive. There were half as many people as I had seen years before, but the noise was greater. There were new games and so a new appearance to the fair. There was only one hurling field and many long tables on which men played *fidchell*.† Only a few vendors sold the old wares: baskets, cheese, cakes, and such. The fair was now dominated by the trading of livestock, and the ground was bare from being trampled by horses, pigs, cattle, and goats. Indeed, I could no longer call this a fair but a place to procure husbanded animals. As I walked through the stalls and bargaining groups, the smell of manure heavy around me, I saw no gleemen nor heard any jin-

---

*Teách Duinn: an island southwest of Ireland where the dead are said to gather.
†*Fidchell*: a game like chess.

gling of bells or trumpet. I stopped to listen to one woman play the harp. Her slender fingers moved gracefully over the instrument and made it sing as I imagine a spirit sings to express its loneliness in the deep forest where there is a sweet longing. The music drew out tears, and I was glad when she stopped, though now I think it was the most beautiful sound I have heard except for the sound of Giannon's low voice as I heard it with my ear pressed against his chest.

I felt sick from the smells and dust and from the yelling of the men who announced with agitating repetition the strength of their animals. Small as I was, my pack and I were knocked upon by shoulder and arm as men competed for the best view of a bull or a horse. I set out for the oak trees under which the druids sat, in hopes of finding familiar poets and astrologers with whom to talk. I was afraid that they would scorn or curse me for my association with the man who had not kissed their brows. I was afraid, too, that I would see in their faces a hideous pity that came from their knowledge of Giannon's fate. They would turn from me rather than tell me of their memories of his screams as his heart ceased to beat and he succumbed to some unjust and cold cruelty. To believe that those we love did not die in contortions of pain is all we humans can do to comfort ourselves when death has separated us forever. It is a pitiful solace, and when we cannot have it we say that death was merciful in ending their torment. God have mercy on us.

There were no druids that year at the oak tree. Instead there were four tonsured men, monks who called out words about Our Lord Jesus Christ when anyone passed. I watched them as I stood behind a group of women with their children. I studied the monks' words and the responses of the people who walked by. No one scorned them. Many lowered their heads and walked on, dragging behind them their hoofed bargains.

I interrupted the women, who looked at my pack with curiosity and amusement. I asked them where and when the council of women was to meet. One, whose face was lined as though spiders had made webs on it, cleared the phlegm from her throat with a hard sound and said, "There is no council of women here. It has not met for four years. Not here has it met, not where it could be known who was meeting." Her lips curled up in a smile, but I could see in her eyes that she was not merry. The women then began a conversation about the council of women, which I listened to well, and they asked me to tell them a good story. I told them about the Glen of Lunatics, where the *geìlt** of Leinster went. The old woman said that I was a good *ban-druí*,†️ but she mixed her admiration with pity and looked with agitation at one of the women in the group who wore a cross around her neck. The woman who wore the cross put her fingers into a pouch on her belt and brought out a silver circle, which she pressed into my hand. She said, "This is for the story you entertained us with." That was the first *screpull*‡️ I ever held, and I liked well the picture on it,

---

*Geìlt: one who goes mad and flees from battle.
†️Ban-druí: female druid.
‡️Screpull: silver coin.

which was of the head of a man. The women laughed when I held the coin up and turned it about in the sunlight. The old woman said, "You can trade that for cheese, or *bairgen,* or cloth." Now she grinned and seemed merry even in her eyes. Since then I have seen many coins and heard them jingle in men's pockets.

The monks around the oak tree called out to the people of the fair to be baptized. The women nodded their heads to me and moved on. Then I saw that one of the monks had a face I had seen before. I filled up with excited happiness when I saw that it was the face of Mongan, the monk who had come home one night with Giannon many years before. I went up to him, and he saw directly who I was and embraced me. Here I put down my pack of scrolls in the dust at the feet of these monks and held the hands of the one I knew. He looked behind me, and I knew that he expected to see Giannon. My tears fell as they had when I heard the music of the harp, for I had hoped Mongan had good news about Giannon. And now here in the world of trade and conversation I felt very keenly the absence of the man whose companionship I had thought to have all of my days. It had been easier to endure his absence in the silence of our home, broken only by the rustlings of creatures and breezes and the near and far howling of wolves. For it seemed a blasphemy to me that men and women continued to laugh and bargain when Giannon and I had been separated, causing me a deep sorrow that I felt the world should share.

I pulled Mongan to the edge of the woods and, still holding both of his hands lest he dissolve like a twilight vision, told him of the night that Giannon had disappeared. He was silent then, but still we clutched one another like children in the wind. I asked to stay some days with him, for I suddenly felt the weakness of my spirit.

In those days, the monk Mongan told me of the comfort he received from Our Lord Jesus Christ. He prayed for me and for Giannon. I heard prayers and scriptures in his circle of monks and was well liked for my desire to learn Latin. The night when the vendors packed their leavings and drank all the mead and cider that remained, I listened to Mongan's advice. He said that he understood well from Giannon and from observing me that I had great talents in reading and writing. He told me plainly that Christ, who suffered for the weak by being affixed to wooden beams like the skin of an animal put out to dry, loved me well and had given me these talents to be used in his service, to comfort the souls of the people of this land. He showed me a picture of Christ on the cross, a light around his head and deep sorrow and patience in his eyes. I asked, "And this man rose up in his tomb like a man stretching after sleep?" And he answered, "Yes, with the wounds from his suffering still on his body." He told me also that the Christians had in their possession a number of scrolls and manuscripts as I had never dreamed could exist, with writings from places that took many fortnights to reach by land and water. God provided the men and women who served Him with an infinite amount of parchment and ink. Mongan's words became a vision to me. I was lifted beyond my own story to hear of places beyond even Britain, of which I knew a little, and to hear of places bigger than a chieftain's lodge, full of parchment and tablets on which the words of many dead men were written and could be read. All this I wanted to tell Giannon.

I added to my pack some of the scrolls the monks had and returned to Giannon's hut to see it changed only by cobwebs and the teeth marks and droppings of mice. I waited still for Giannon to return, but another year went by, during which his garden became ragged and chaotic, and the wolves came near at night and I wept with them for the hardships of the world. I tried to find signs in the patterns of clouds, in the direction of the stars that arced across the sky, in the hum that sometimes came at night and made the world tremble. I read the ripples in the pools and dared to kneel as the monks had knelt and asked for the voice of their god to speak to me. To what was I to be devoted? What was the more solid vision—this god who stood up from his sepulcher or Giannon's return? Was there no other thing more real or more present to occupy my existence? How many times had I hoped for things beyond my small power to acquire, such as the comfort of my dead mother or the growth of a child in my womb? Was my wish to be a druid, free and unattached to chieftain or *túath,* another wisp of straw to be blown from my small hands? I had seen at Tailltenn the position druids were now given in the land and wondered if they would take up their place again. I calculated the possibility that the tonsured men would leave so that I could have the privilege I had thought of when I first determined to be Giannon's apprentice. But I had seen the number of monks increase and the derision they received decrease. Each *túath* in turn converted, though I had heard that in remote areas, the pagans still went to the stone rings. I had seen chieftains' warriors accompany the tonsured men and stand guard beside them.

One devotion stayed with me, and it was to a power I had in my own hands and my own head. The power of words seemed worthy of complete faith and did not betray or trick me. Words were visible, the stones with which all stories and laws were built. All stories, whether about the great battles of Cuchulain or the great miracles of Christ, relied on words. I was sure of their strength and value as I could be sure of nothing else. They had been a solid and tangible part of my life, reaching back into my mother's purse of pebbles and back further through the tales of my ancestors. I had no need to plead with gods or mortals to make marks as long as there were sticks, or my own fingers, as long as I had a voice that could form the sounds either to others or in my own head. I acknowledge the source of my talent as bigger than my own insignificant self. I also believe that I was meant to use my words for truth telling and not for some political purpose or to raise my own position. I pray that my truth telling be understood as a service to God and that He will forgive my confusion and ignorance.

Giannon metamorphosed in my mind into a spirit whose influence I could sometimes feel like a breeze on my neck. I heard his practical advice and considered that I might be valued as a bard with the many scrolls I possessed, both pagan and Christian. I would offer knowledge as others offer meat or wine. I might even find a boy or girl as stricken with a love of knowledge as I was and teach what I knew. I chose to travel south, though I was afraid of the wildness there. I chose to go in front of the wave of Christians to where a druid's skills were not scorned or challenged. My purpose in traveling to the south was also to look for Giannon or any news of him. I reasoned with hope.

In those times omens came with the strength of a mallet on the head. I was followed by a decrepit she-wolf from Giannon's dwelling, all the way to the woods that edged the *túath* of Tarbfhlaith. Her sad but protective presence matched the ruin of the *túath* that I had been born into, a ruin so thorough that the remains of my own father's home was a hill on which grass grew. I had been gone many years from that place and reasoned that it had stayed as I had known it, that the children would still be children and the number of pigs neither more nor less. I wanted to have peace one time in the place where my child's body had been filled with storms. I wanted to serve what kin I had their cups of ale and their meat before I left on my solitary travels. But I saw no human and only a few wild pigs, who fled into the woods when I stepped near them. I saw only what humans had made and left, a few remnants to show that this had been a *dal*.* The pens and huts had long ago fallen, and grasses grew around the wood they had been made of. The paths of mud between the huts were carpeted with grass

---

Dal: land where a tribe exists.

[143]

and thistle. There was no boat at the lake and only two poles still standing to which boats had once been tethered. A thrush sat on the very tip of one of the poles and spoke to me in its language.

I picked up a *bas-chrann** as though I might strike it on an invisible door and be let into the chieftain's hut. I could see the boundaries of the *bàdhum* † and the green and lush grass there, fertilized by the manure of cattle long gone. I sat inside a *dabhach*‡ that was perched on a mound. I rested my arms on its edges and looked over the *túath* of Tarbfhlaith, which was no more. I then realized that what men fight for is not permanent. When or why Tarbfhlaith was abandoned I did not know. But I have heard since that a plague overcame the place and killed the majority there, including the chieftain and his kin. I cried for my older sister and lay certain plants on the mound where our dwelling had been, in case her spirit and those of her children were there. I thought of the face of my younger sister, who would have been a young woman and whose whereabouts I know nothing of even to this day, though I try to believe that she left Tarbfhlaith unharmed by the plague. And I wondered then if either druid or Christian were to blame for the ruin of Tarbfhlaith, or if it be attributed to the power that is beyond all doctrine and ritual. What power that is I cannot say, nor do I believe that there is a name for it. It occupies

---

*Bas-chrann: small wooden log used as a knocker.

†*Bàdhum*: place where cows are kept.

‡*Dabhach*: two-handled tub.

the place where my beloved words cannot go, where they fall like pebbles in the ocean.

I learned regret in the ruins of Tarbfhlaith. I regretted that ambition had ruled my heart instead of affection for my kin. And with the lesson of regret came the gratitude for having life still to move my lips and limbs, and to speak kind words to and embrace those I may not see again on this sweet-smelling earth. I learned that I cannot wait to love what is in my presence, for it or I may well be gone tomorrow. To some, such as Giannon, this lesson poisons the heart with bitterness. But such bitterness has no value and is, in fact, cowardly. For bitterness risks nothing.

So began in lonely circumstances my *Baile Shuibhe*.* I had no kin, no companion in gleemen or husband, druid or monk. The decrepit she-wolf stayed with me for a season, and I believed that she was my mother overseeing my journey, though now I am told that we do not return in other forms but have only one incarnation. The wolf, having become more frail than fearful, ate from my hands, and I gave her what I could without starving myself. I spoke to her, and she listened and looked into my eyes. I wept against her fur, clutching her thin body that stumbled in its effort to let me lean against her. She lay one morning panting, her eyes gazing at death, and I held her and stroked her fur. I told her she had been a fine wolf and that she would soon be free to perfect her soul in another form. At the edge of win-

---

Baile Shuibhe: frenzy of Sweeny, who went in search of peace of mind by developing an animal familiarity with nature.

ter the wolf died, providing me with a warm skin. I let her body empty itself of her spirit and then took the warm skin to wear as a cloak. The need to survive dominated all other ideas and philosophies. I do not hunt well, but my smallness allowed me to hide and my knowledge allowed me to frighten other animals with fire or curses. I sometimes chased wolves away from their kill and ate good meat cooked over a fire. In loneliness I spoke to animals and trees, as my mother had done, and I saw the living spirit in blades of grass and felt the affection of the rain on my face. Perhaps I was mad. But I lived thoroughly, seeing and hearing and feeling and tasting for my mother and Giannon and for the wolf as well, and for the drowned *oblaire* and for all those whose death or suffering had smothered their senses. And while fulfilling my obligations to the dead, I looked for my place in the world.

When I was in the mountains, I cut the boughs of evergreens to cover myself with in the night. I tried to stop thinking of my longing and dread, quieting my thoughts by watching the clouds change form, but in every place I stayed I left signs of my devotion to the two I had loved so strongly. I will not dwell on the tedium of this time in my life. These years are full of the repetition of the procurement and consumption of food, though I will tell of the instances when I had more revelations and learned of the lands to the south in those times.

I came sometimes to a *túath,* but none so wealthy as to want knowledge more than help with sowing and grinding. The druids in those parts traveled from *túath* to *túath* and were often themselves herdsmen, having no great halls to languish in while entertaining chieftains. Indeed, the chieftains in those parts were set apart from all other men by no clear costume or power, but by small things such as owning a horse or wearing a brooch. I told my stories and was generously fed, but could not stay long in one *túath* without being pressed to become a man's wife or servant or to move on. Few had heard of the Christians other than rumors of Pelagians. In one place I found a ring of stones where human sacrifice had recently occurred. A boy's bones, it was said, had been crushed to fit inside an urn and buried in the center of the circle. The people who knew of this stone circle looked away or hid their faces with their hair when I asked the identity of the boy and the significance of his martyrdom. I wondered if he were their Jesus Christ who died for their suffering and was in heaven preparing their way to Paradise. But a boy whose bones are crushed and put in an urn has little chance of getting up and walking about again. In that place I felt some danger and moved on.

Once I traded my ability to transcribe law for a pair of goats. Then I was a herdsman and a nomad. I fed from the milk and cheese the goats provided and gave what I did not need to others who were hungry. When the female was old I slaughtered her for meat, kindly telling her first, as is pagan custom, that her life was of great value and that it would be used with gratitude. In our ignorance, the people of this land thanked the animal whose meat we ate and not God, for it seemed that the animal made the greater sacrifice.

I traveled as herdsman for several years, during which

time the scrolls became a burden to me and I burned them for fuel. There were times of illness and rough challenges. Once a bear knocked me down from behind and sat on me, breathing on my neck with breath that was warm and foul as though the beast had had its own feces as a meal. It left me unmolested, but I dreamed that night that it spoke to me and said that I had best go north again. I left those remote and wild parts with visions that I still return to for comfort. Those lands rumble with a large beauty of varying colors and heights. I cannot see that any religion is true that does not recognize its gods in the green wave of trees on a mountainside or the echo of a bird's song that makes ripples on a shadowed pool. Even in the quick snap of a hare's neck and the gleam of living in the eyes of the fox whose mouth is full of the hare's fur, there is God, even though He is not understood. This land is full of holiness that I cannot describe. Brigit knows this. Brigit to me is the wisest of all the saints. She knows the value of ale and the comfort of poetry.

TENTH INTERRUPTION

SAINT BRIGIT protect us from suspicion and chaos. All manner of drama has occurred here that claws at the peace I begged to join. I would rather be in the southern woods where moss grows thick over stone pillars and reeds shudder as fish swim between them in dark pools. But I can only travel there in words and recollection, for my legs ache too much now for wandering. And I am tired when I think of days of hungry solitude. The times I have loved most were days and nights of repeated and unremarkable peace when I made a good broth and saw Giannon's stained shoe step onto the threshold; or when I watched the goats graze on grasses glowing with the light that exists in every blade. A tiny translucent spider once made a web between my fingers while I slept, an act of trust performed by a tender creature who wanted nothing more than to sustain itself. I knew when I awoke not to move my hand too carelessly, even before I saw the tiny presence there. Now there is more complication, and I have been unwise. I mean no harm to any soul, but I am sometimes careless with my opinions. My words have pricked the ears of people who resent and want to silence them. I feel sick and compelled to leave this sanctuary, may Brigit help me. And where will I go?

I have bitter sorrow for the abbot, who has been bedridden for three days. On the first day of his affliction he sent a young monk to me who requested transcription of the Book of Revelation, in which it is written, *Foris canes et venefici et impudici et homicidae.*[*] I have heard that this monk took the parchment with the ink not yet dry to the abbot's sickbed, where the abbot underwent surgery performed by another monk, who butchers our meat. This surgery, Sister Luirrenn has told me, is of the worst and most unspeakable kind, and I now suspect with strong conviction that this place has a foul madness in it, and that indeed every god, even the new one, weeps for our misguided and unnecessary agonies. Mimicking Origen, our abbot has castrated himself, and he says it is to ensure his own purity. We all pray for him, Sister Aillenn with a quiet piety that is unusual in its serenity. She looks at me above her clasped hands, and when our eyes meet, she shows me her strength. The nuns do not speak of this act or their opinion of it, and I am sick with the thought of it and have beat my own breast to think of it and of the thing of which he has accused me, as though darkness and mutilation are his creeds.

On this, the third day after his martyrdom, I was called to come to the abbot where he lay. His face was most pale, and I think he will die. His lips were white and dry as he spoke to me. He said that he had had many visions as he

---

[*]"Outside are dogs and sorcerers and whores and murderers."

lay in fever and pain. God had come to him in many forms and with many voices, some low and some as loud as the thunder that quickly follows lightning. With persistence, God has told him that among the sisters there is a witch so foul that she eats the flesh of infants. He closed his eyes and said to me that three times it was I who had found the grave molested and finally empty. He said also that he knows that I go with laywomen to the woods to perform rituals and gather plants. Fiercely and on my knees I begged him to hear me and know my innocence. I begged him to search my cell and find no evil accessories there, nor any sign of demonic practice. He spoke with detail of the foul act of eating the infant's corpse; imagining the white grave worms in my mouth, I fled from him.

I saw Sister Aillenn peering out at me from her *clochan* as I passed, her eyes round and still, and I remembered that she called me *bean sidhe*. She followed me to my cell, her calmness apparent and unusual. When I turned to look upon her face, she took my hand, which was cold with terror. She whispered, "A sacrifice has been made," and stared long into my eyes with merry looks, as though she held back laughter. She further said, "My beauty can no longer compel him to succumb to demons." When I asked that she leave me, she sat on my writing stool and looked through the parchment there. She said, "I will find out who has more power, you or he." I answered her that I wanted no power but only peace. But she said that I was beloved by the people and good at flinging the truth in a man's face as a druid does by whispering it onto a blade of grass and throwing it at his enemy. I told Sister Aillenn that I had no enemies and that the druid tricks were only as powerful as the fear they caused. Her madness now seems a melting snow, revealing beneath it a ground full of stones. I am afraid that she has transferred her affliction to me, for as she grows more lucid, I grow more confused by what I am accused of, for I have neither youth nor wealth nor kin nor husband to ward off harm.

Sister Luirrenn has been kind to me, telling me to stay in my cell and not attend the daily masses, so as to keep out of sight. I am sorry to stay away from the singing of psalms and find that my cell grows smaller when I cannot walk to the woods and on the hills. Twice flowers have been left at my door whose fragrance is fair and welcome to me, the sweet harebell and yellow cowslip. And I saw the second time the monk who does not speak walking from my *clochan*, his straw hat and wild beard fluttering with his hurried steps; his stride is long and his back straight. And because I am succumbing to the chaos of this troubled convent, I believed that this gait belonged to Giannon. I fell to my knees, gasping and weeping to God, "Let it be Giannon come to take me home." And the sound of his name and of the word *home* reached so deeply into my flesh that the sobs shook my body. I tried to construct in my mind the face of Giannon beneath the silent monk's hat and beard, and yet could not even clearly see that face in memory. I could only hear his voice in a certain phrase or glimpse his mouth in a certain configuration. But the whole of his person had been lost to me like a clay pot that has shattered so that one can only hold pieces of its design. And what would it mean if Giannon had come to this place and not made himself known to me? What new pain would be in my bones, to find that he did not remember me or did not care to speak to me? Would it be better to believe that he ignores me or to admit, for the thousandth time, that he was long ago killed in a manner I should not even guess at, taken from my sight forever, no matter how much I longed for him, just as my mother had become a painful silence? It seems better to me to see the corpse and know that the spirit in it is gone, for there is no doubt to those who have touched and looked upon the dead that there is no one there. But hope that someone is still alive or that a beloved's coldness will end becomes its own corpse, hung around the neck with a stink from which the bearer cannot part. My hope that Giannon had come to coddle me at this most treacherous time was cruel. And what need did I have of Giannon or anyone else to move me from this place? Could I not walk of my own will and on my own tired legs from this place and go again into the wilderness with goats and wits? The thought made my knees and ankles ache with a dread of having no home when I have had this one for five years. I am a wanderer no more. I want only to sit alone in my *clochan* and read and write, bent over parchments.

Dear Brigit, who protects and inspires poets, could I not be left alone, a barren woman, to scratch marks on parchment with innocent devotion to wisdom? I pity and then scold myself for being like a child crying for its mother's breast. There is no one whose life is not hard in this land, no one who is not weary. I feel the weariness of all the people of this land, which sometimes pulls me to my bedding even when the bell rings for psalms. But I also know the joyful spirit of the people of the *túaths*, who feed fairies and love feasts. And I wonder what the men who love the potency of the bull would say about a man who takes the power from between his legs and discards it as refuse. What is this shame concerning the pleasure-loving bodies God gave us? What is this sin that is original in our flesh? Perhaps shame is the greatest sin, worse than any other. May God forgive me, or not. I now wonder if the people who grow flax and raise pigs and tell stories of the Hound of Culann should cast out the foreign-born who shame themselves and others. We should take their improvements, discarding the rest. On my knees I bow my head, for I am afraid of my blasphemous anger that seems like truth. I see Christ upon the cross, a black sky swirling above his bent head, and I beg him to open his eyes and look at me.

The wind whips the world outside as though to strike at a beast who will not carry its burden. The wind also brings pieces of the singing of psalms to me. The voice of Sister Aillenn sounds strong today. She is often asked to sing alone, for she mimics the unearthly and harmonious lullaby of an angel who looks down at Our Lord as he suffers and dies on the tree. I think sometimes of His loneliness and of the way in which all time and all places converge in His suffering and weariness, and I want to weep for Him and the world. It is in Jesus' human form that I recognize a hero. He did not hide himself from suffering and doubt. He was fully human. That he rose from the dead is a trick to seduce people who need such tricks. The whole universe, from the darkening sky that reveals the constellations to the light that exists in a beetle's eye, is already trick enough if we are not afraid to contemplate our own smallness in the infinite mystery. But sometimes we are simply hungry and lonely. That Christ fed fish and bread to the poor and spoke to the outcast whore makes me want his company on this dark night. The world is full of immortals but sorely lacking in kindness.

Sister Luirrenn brought food to me in the afternoon and prayed with me. She has told me that the silent monk tends my garden in my place. It is hard punishment to have the work among the herbs and flowers taken away. This night and for the days that follow until I am let again into the company of the sisters, I will continue my story, for now I am at that place where I must tell how I came to the convent of Saint Brigit. And also I will transcribe the codices of scripture, for well I know my duties here, which I have always loved. And when I have finished and said farewell to my sisters, leaving my tears on the backs of their hands, I will go on and make a hut for myself in a *túath* where charity to an old woman is a virtue. For though I look only to be at the end of my youth, I feel instead at the beginning of my old age.

[11]

WHEN I WALKED NORTHWARD, I came along a well-traveled road on which there was a hostel with common room and sleeping corners. The innkeep sold ale there and claimed it was the ale of Brigit miraculously transformed from water. There is no better saint for this land than one who turns water to ale. But I said that I had known Brigit as a god, and the people in that place scorned my ignorance and said that she was a saint now, having been converted by Patrick himself. Some said she was the mother of the hero Jesus. Others said that she was God's wife, or even his female manifestation. Others said she was just a woman who had been raised by a druid and saved from perdition by our first bishop. They told me that this Patrick had done battle with druids and smashed their skulls as though they were birds' eggs. I heard in these stories an old devotion to might and ale and did not feel unfamiliar with the themes though they had new names attached to them. Some told me that when Patrick died, a twelve-day wake was held; all the *túath*s and cultivated lands were filled with the sound of bells and lit by funeral torches. My mother had told me nothing of this, but it is said to be true. The innkeep told me too that a druid had poisoned Patrick's ale, which was made by the saint's own brewer. Here is another aspect of a true saint, a man with his own brewer. I had no hostility toward Patrick, nor do I now, though his Latin is not well formed.

I stayed for over a year at the hostel, partaking of large quantities of the holy ale, which was good. And I thought often that this new religion was not an uncomfortable one. I put aside my sorrow over the Pelagian who had been drowned and my suspicion that Christians had dragged Giannon into the long night of absence. I became a congenial soul among the people who came to the hostel on their way from one market to another or on their way home with their herds. The innkeep used my talents to encourage others to drink his beer. I told stories and wrote legal agreements between men concerning a *cumal** or a marriage arrangement. I saw coins exchanged there in regular and copious amounts and remembered the silver I had been given at the Fair of Tailltenn years before. I was suspicious of a thing that could not be used directly but was a symbol for useful things, so I preferred payment in meat and ale. Sometimes I grew too loud, and more than once I found myself in the pigpen, being doused with water by the innkeep, who was like a brother to me. He might have put me on the road had I not sat beside his wife when she had a

---

**Cumal:* unit of bargaining equaling three milk cows or a certain amount of land.

killing fever and stroked her hand. I listened to her fears and told her that her eyes were beautiful, like the eyes of Queen Mebd, and then she closed those same eyes and stopped living as herself.

On a night when I had fallen down beside the trough, my face and hair in wet dirt, a new voice called my name. I looked up to see Mongan, the monk who had come with Giannon that night long, long ago and whom I had seen at the Fair of Tailltenn in the year of the silver coin. The man's face had grown soft furrows, and he had developed a limp, caused, he said, when he fell one night and the wheel of an ox cart rolled over his leg. I was glad to see him, but he feared for my condition, which was not good or noble. I explained my life with goats and other beasts, refraining from telling the account with the bear, which I had told before and which had become a satire. He understood that I was in some kind of despair, though I myself did not acknowledge it. For a fortnight, the monk Mongan stayed with me and kept the *ballcin** from my hand. I was then stricken with a terrible shaking and a sickness of worms, and I said *Gonomil, organmil, morbumil.*† Mongan told me to leave off these kinds of chants, which were dangerous and evil. He comforted me with the story of Saint Brigit. His words made her form before my eyes as a true sister, for she was raised as a druid and hated suffering. She fed the sick and soon came to know God and Our Lord Jesus Christ, who

---

**Ballcin:* cup or vessel made of wood.
†*Gonomil, organmil, morbumil:* a chant to kill worms.

gave her the power to perform miracles. She could see into a person's soul, and she saw into mine and brought from it the sorrow and rage I felt and turned it into a great weariness that still sometimes sits upon me. Mongan stayed with me through the night when Brigit, whose hair was a dark cloak like my mother's, brought the sorrow and rage out of me. And then I was cured, and there was a peace about me that I had never known. Still, I wanted to know the purpose of my suffering and of the agonies humans endured. Mongan told me that there was another place of solace that one went to after this life. And I am still suspicious of such words that are like coins, representing something useful but not useful in themselves.

I came out of my sickness and asked for parchment, for I wanted to write down the story of Brigit in gratitude for how she had come to me. Mongan told me then that I should go to the convent where Brigit, though she be dead, still came to tend her own sacred flame as a sister to the nuns who guarded that same flame. This vision shone like a brilliant jewel to me. I wanted nothing more than to speak to one who had died and might know the true purpose of our hard lives. And Mongan reminded me of the unlimited stacks of parchment and the tomes, which I could read and transcribe. I said to him, for I wanted always to tell the truth, "What else can I do but be a *cele dé?* What else but drown in ale and immortalize laws that concern the ownership of pigs and spoons?" For I was neither wife nor druid. I had no husband, no child, and no knowledge of where the powerful *aes dána* had hidden themselves. I remembered, too, that Giannon himself had told me that the most complete store of knowledge, which included histories from faraway lands and times, was in the convents and monasteries.

I thought many days and nights about the hero Jesus and prayed with Mongan to understand Him. I saw one night the eyes of Our Lord as they had looked when He was bolted to the tree. His eyes were weary but made of compassion. I smelled His sweat and tasted the blood that fell down His face from the thorns. And He smiled at me, as though we shared an understanding that time passed and that one legend took the place of another as one chieftain dies and another slips onto his seat of power and marries the land. I asked the monk Mongan about the social position of nuns, and he told me that they were like poets, coming after guests but before musicians at a banquet. He said that some nuns were young, some old, and that some were women who were wives to other women. He told me that there were women who were elders and acted as mothers to the other women. I told Mongan that I would become one of God's devoted at Brigit's church. I combed my hair and brushed my cloak and traveled on the road to Kildare with a scroll signed and sealed by Mongan attesting to my pure intentions.

I was then living in weariness and well ready to find a home and useful vocation. My mind was like an empty cup. I let no thoughts of my old life pour into it. When I came to Kildare, I saw there a long building on the hill, surrounded by small hives made of stone that are the *clochan*s we live in. At the bottom of the hill were the houses of the laypeople. I passed these by and came to the chapel, which had no human in it. Inside I saw the flame and heard my own breath and my own heartbeat in that large structure that was like a rich chieftain's hall. Then Sister Luirrenn found me. I fell onto the floor before her and asked to come among the sisters. She asked if I were baptized, and I said yes, which was a lie that I have not repented.

I do not want to be a liar to Sister Luirrenn, who has been so good to me. It was she to whom I showed the scroll written by Mongan and my own scrolls as well. She welcomed and blessed me. I sang loudly and ran in the garden and around each *clochan,* feeling blessed freedom from the uncertainty of where I would go and what I would do. I was in ecstasy to think that I had come to a place, and been let into it, where a human who had died could tell me what death is and therefore what life is. I wanted to stay by Brigit's flame, to do nothing but wait for her and hear her tell me all that I needed to know. And I promised her in my thoughts that I would tell others only what she allowed me to tell them, and that if she did allow such a messenger, I would endure briar patches and roads turned to lakes to alleviate the ignorance of any humans I could reach. The scrolls and tablets and codices that I saw before me intoxicated me more thoroughly than all the innkeep's ale. I envisioned a profound blessing of understanding disease, pain, old age, and death, a blessing every human hungers for no matter how much meat is on his platter. I wondered that I could use my druid skills to write these truths on parchment. And I also knew, without planning it, that I would make immortal with all the parchment and ink available to me those whom I loved and was never to see again. I have wanted to write the truth, but I still do not have the wisdom for the task.

I have not yet seen Brigit or heard her voice. But I have had ideas come into my mind that seem like wisdom. For one, I agree with the Pelagians, though I be found out and my head held under the water of some brown lake for heresy; all that God has made is sacred, but in ways that the human cannot understand with thoughts but must know in the moment between breaths. Such a notion has blossomed from the seed sown when I went to the woods with my mother. Mongan asked me once if I had not considered that to the Pelagians worms are sacred since they are created by God. And I said then that perhaps in suffering worms we are made to be more grateful for pleasure. I know that to be human is to suffer. But even suffering can be sacred if it compels one to give and receive kindness and to despise harmful acts.

I have learned many things since I came to Brigit's chapel and read the letters and scriptures of the saints. I will give here the sum of the facts I have seen concerning the transformation in this land since Christians have come here, in case they not be recorded by any other hand:

1st, *improvements in tools and methods used for husbandry*
2nd, *increase in varieties and hardiness of plants and domestic animals*

[163]

3rd, *decrease in violence between* túaths *and in the taking of hostages*

4th, *increase in literacy and knowledge of the world*

5th, *increase in the distance between the rich and the poor, the latter increasing in numbers while the former increase in wealth*

6th, *decrease in the influence and freedom of women, whose councils exist no longer and whose property has been diminished*

7th, *increase in cruelty to the land and disregard for its power and beauty*

I see the improvements the Christians have brought, but these improvements and payments in gold have seduced the chieftains away from powers older and more elemental than scripture. The chieftains themselves relied too much on druids for their knowledge and did not make themselves wise enough. Surely a wise leader would see the benefits of marrying old wisdom to new devices, of scorning intolerance and dogma while embracing the new heroes and rituals, which have such pretty sounds and good influence. I would live in a world full of Christ-like humans, but not one full of Christians, may God forgive me. This I can now say as I prepare to leave this place, having reached the truth of my own limitations as a follower of the Christian doctrine, which the abbot has shown to be fertile ground for harmful shame and fear.

I have seen that the Christian philosophy of the bishops compels people to turn away from the earth and toward heaven. It encourages a view of earth as a place of degradation and temptation and spreads this view of our one mother to include all mothers, whose wombs are considered unclean. And it seems curious to me that those who condemn this earth and its goods most vehemently and greedily amass those goods. The monks who preach and practice poverty are exceptions to the priests and converted chieftains who instead practice fierce and jealous acquisition. Then these rich men confess and say certain words to garner absolution for the sins they committed in order to become wealthy. But they keep the wealth. The chieftains who used to know the earth as their wife now use her as mistress. I fear that the cleverest means of power will be for the Christians to use their wealth to own the weapons and war beasts that will give them dominance over the distribution of grain and land. This, I have heard, has already happened in Britain, where the priests have armies to mete out their doctrines and have made the people so dependent on them that they give portions of their harvests to them. It is no mystery that the Pelagians and others who say that a man can speak directly to God without a priest have been discovered floating in lakes and sleeping with axes in their skulls. Power does not willingly give up its place to truth, though I thought it would. I did not understand. May God and all who read this forgive me if my words are heresy. I still love the power of words. They dispel my loneliness. They soothe my fear of uselessness.

But I say that wind and water or fire and worms can overcome any words or theory, and some priests would do well to be humbled by this fact. They would do well to look away from their manuscripts and icons from time to time. But I understand their need to dwell on miracles, codes, and saints. With me it is not so much piety as loneliness that makes me beg the hero Jesus or Brigit or any god or saint to appear to me so I can believe and feel protected, even if they do not tell me for what purpose the world exists. How sorely I need to feel that words and stories do not disguise chaos and disaster but hint at some comforting wisdom. How well I understand the true torment of hell as being eternally kept from seeing the face of God. I already know this punishment, but it is, I confess, perhaps an exile of my own doing. How thorough the loneliness! How tiresome the self-pity! I wish that I could thoroughly believe in some creed. I wish that I was ignorant enough to know one truth and discard all others.

As time passes and the abbot lies with his legs spread to comfort his wound, I have been forgotten here. There is neither punishment nor absolution concerning my suspected devilry. I have become invisible. Only Sister Aillenn came to tell me that the abbot has risen from his bed and, though he walks slowly and winces often, hears confession and gives sermon in the chapel. She touched the pages on which I make marks, staring at them and saying that they look like worm trails. She said that she took my place guarding the flame when it was my turn to do so. Such news made me suffer and tempted me to walk in the night hoping not to be seen. I went to the dwellings of the laypeople, where I saw the woman whose infant was buried here, and she hid her face with her hair. So pitiful was her sorrow and shame that I promised to give her comfort and speak well of her in my prayers to Brigit. She has no living child and her husband has taken a young woman as his wife to bear him children. I combed her hair. I saw also the monk who has taken my place as gardener, and I was stricken with rage. I saw him as a fool in a frayed hat and unruly beard.

Restlessness abides. I feel like the horse who smells the storm though the sky is blue.

One more night of sleep and I will make a plan to move on, for in the end I am a pagan or heretic more than one of these Christians, and I see no reason for the authority of the men called bishops and popes other than the hats they wear, as foolish as the hat of the mute gardener. I should not use this place and these good women any longer. The abbot may well know that I am a weed amid the flax, and he, unlike my sweet sisters, will not suffer imperfection.

LAST ENTRY

I AM OLD TODAY. And I am just born. I am a bird, or a fox, or a bowl, or a knife. These words say it, but they cannot make it so. I can tell you that I have flown this night and seen the face of God and that it looked like the moon almost full. I can tell you that I have grown as small as a piece of threshed grain and fell through a tiny hole in a sieve and that a mouse will eat me soon. Words can say these things, and that is all. The word is not made flesh except in some tale. And what rod do you use to measure the truth of words? What *fé**** to lay against the words and see that flesh fits them? Use your own organs and senses as *fé*.

I have time to write many truths, including what has happened here at the Order of Saint Brigit on the holiest of nights. I have time and opportunity to do no other thing but transcribe scriptures, prayers, letters, and truths because my ankles are chained by irons to a heavy stake that has been pounded deep into the earth in my cell. In this way has the nun Gwynneve finally been made an immovable

---

*Fé: stick used to measure a person's grave.

servant of God. I could begin to wail, a beast on its tether whose night screams would call out either pity or hatred. Such screams, like the ones I heard from Sister Aillenn's cell, always come to us at night from a distance or from behind a wall or from inside a neighbor's dwelling. One listens or one covers one's ears, perhaps praying that the tormented sounds stop. And when they do stop, the world is silent and hangs its head. There is no purpose in wailing unless one is a child who must be found by his mother. I am not lost. My mother is lost. She is lost in death as we all are when we travel there, even in our thoughts.

The accusations against me grow hideous. It is said that I have hidden things in my body in unclean orifices and that I entice children and demons to extract them and engage in foul orgies. It is said that I have lust for corpses and the ability to transform myself. Where is the reason for this? For if I could transform myself, would I not grow wings and fly far away? I would turn my swollen ankles into birds' legs and hop through the doorway. Bending and then lifting in an exquisite moment of release, I would feel the spread of my beautiful black wings and the freedom of the vast sky.

My imprisonment began a few days before the twentieth night of the cycle of Brigit, when I made many prayers to many gods and spirits, flinging supplications out like feed for pigs. And whichever god consumed whichever prayer, I wished him to be pleased and give me comfort and grace and power over my fears. I was sick with a need for godly hand or voice as proof that my soul did not drift in empty space. When I looked out at the frozen mud and heard the psalms coming from the cold chapel, I felt the chill of emptiness and silence beneath all things, as though the world were a woven carpet slung over black ice. I had evil visions of the toothless gap in Sister Luirrenn's mouth and of the bloodied indentation between the abbot's legs. I saw, in this horrible mural, the thread of blood on my mother's lips, the bruises on Sister Aillenn's arms, the corpse of the stranger who had frozen to death in the forest as he leaned against a tree for rest. And I saw the refusal to give affection, so many times witnessed and felt, as hard as a blow from an oaken club. I was afraid of the evil done in this world, by seen and unseen hands. I was afraid that the lesson I would finally learn was that truth is weaker than greedy power, and that death is the highest power, which causes even an infant to swell and stink. Punished for my hubris in calling myself the teller of truth, I would be shown that I was indeed small. These fears turned to terror, and I could no longer sit and wait in my cell.

Having no sign of intervention from immortals, I went straightaway to the abbot with an appeal, still addicted to my belief that any man will finally honor the truth and reward integrity. Did it not occur to me that for a man to recognize and reward integrity he must first have it himself? Such was my pride, to think that all people of intelligence believed what I believed. I was a fool whose clever mouth spewed forth the chains that would bind me, learning the power of words in a new way. For this abbot wanted control, not wisdom or honor. I went to him both as a child and a warrior, switching roles like the gleeman who paints one side of his face with the mask of a hero and the other with the mask of a hag so that he may play either role by simply turning his head.

I first told the abbot with humble supplication that I wanted to be with the other nuns again before leaving the convent to lead a humbler life. I wanted to eat my meals with my sisters and serve God and Brigit by attending the flame on my assigned night of vigilance. The abbot was still pale and moved stiffly. His mood was cold, and he said that I was an arrogant woman whose head was held too high. He said that I was not humble but aggressive with my talents and that the people in the lay houses came to me for things for which they should seek help from God through a priest such as himself. He said loudly, "What foul actions were started when the woman brought the dying infant to you instead of having it baptized! These old ways clutch at the Church's throat like a mad crone who will strangle it if her hands are not torn away and she is not impaled." I made a terrible error then. I felt my anger and wore it like a chieftain's cloak. I became clever and thought to check him in the battle he had begun. I told the abbot that I knew who had taken the infant and why, and that I did not want harm to come to her but was following Christ's example in protecting the meek, who shall, it is said, inherit the earth. He asked me to tell the person's name, and I said I would not, for it would do no good to bring harm to this person but would be better to pray for the person's tormented soul. He said that sin must be absolved officially, not by a withering pagan woman such as myself. In anger, I asked him, "Has your sin with Aillenn been officially absolved?"

He did not strike me or grow pale or red. He smiled and said nothing. He moved his legs together as though feeling the absence there and receiving confidence from it. The anger drained from me, and I felt instead a pity that was firmer than the anger. I saw then, as I should have seen before, the immense and mysterious damage that this man must have suffered in his life. I saw in his face and in his self-mutilation a surrender to confusion so horrible and so human, so potent in all of us, that I had to understand him. He is like a comrade who has fallen beside me in battle. His weakness can be pitied but must not be ignored. One cannot pretend that such a man is still able to lead us. It is noble to pity a man who is cruel because he is weak, but it is idiotic and dangerous to allow him to have power. I said to him without anger, "You should go from here. If coming has caused you to mutilate yourself, then your coming was an error." He spoke then, saying, "We will play this out, you and I. We will play this out. See what you can do, Gwynneve. I have heard of your visions, of your madness in seeing fornicators, and of the visions you record on parchment. See what you can do, perhaps renouncing your visions and burning your parchments, and bringing the demon who took the dead infant for punishment."

I left feeling a weakness in my legs. And soon after, when I was in my cell, Sister Luirrenn came in with the chains. She read from a scroll, "Sister Gwynneve, you have been accused of defiling graves and consuming human flesh, of consorting with demons and performing pagan rituals with other women, whose ignorance of scripture has made them your victims." I did not argue or struggle against the chains, and I saw that she wept as she secured them to my ankles. The other sisters gathered outside my cell and peered in to see my degradation. But they wrung their hands and called out blessings to me, some in the name of Christ, some in other, more ancient names. Sister Aillenn came to sit on the floor at my feet. I only said to Sister Luirrenn, "Please, Mother, do not take my writing tools." Am I not still a child? Forgive me.

At that time my ankles were chained to each other so that I was able to walk with small and awkward steps. I was afraid at first to go out in the dark, but there were comforts left on my threshold from the garden and from the afternoon meal, indicating that there were those who loved me. I stood in the doorway and watched the backs of the people who furtively left these gifts, some from the lay dwellings. The woman whose infant had begun the trouble came close to the doorway and stood away from me as though afraid. The smell of manure came from her even at that distance. She hid her face with her hair and threw a small bundle of hemlock at my feet. I looked long at the delicate white flowers and dark leaves that hide so well the painful but quick death inside them. With this pretty poison death seduces the melancholic warrior. I do not know whether she gave this to me as vengeance or mercy. Wafting about my door was also the old monk who does not speak. And soon I came to know that he was Giannon, though I had certainty of nothing and desire for everything. He turned to me briefly at dusk on the night of Saint Brigit and looked into my eyes. And when I spoke, saying, "Giannon?," he nodded and went away before the water in his eyes could spill over and before I could feast on his appearance.

Here then seemed to be the sum of my wishes. Of all those who were dead to me, whom I prayed to see again, Giannon was the one I had wanted most. Though my ankles were bound and I was chained as a devil, I felt as though my head had burst open and birds were flying freely from it to the sky. Here was a man, my twin, come to life, resurrected after many years. I could not conceive of it without many hours of breathless pacing and talking to myself. But there were questions enough. Why did he not speak to me? Why had he been here for many weeks and not revealed himself to me and told me what he hoped? I wondered what maimed condition he had been left in by his captors, or if his spirit had been somehow mangled so that he had little reason or will left. Would I rather that he were dead? I sat still for so many hours that the one good candle I had left to me became a mound of wax, the wick drowned.

This was a bitter night. I had always thought that, were Giannon ever to come to me, he would guide all my actions and free all my sorrows. I had to remember instead that love was not easy with Giannon. And even with this man who understood my strengths, I was always alone. Perhaps this is the knowledge I had refused to put in my mouth and swallow since my mother had died. This is the wisdom that

Giannon had always made plain to me and that he still represents with his great silence—that I am Gwynneve alone. Well I should know this lesson, for I have sat beside the dying and understand the limitations of any companionship. There is a place on the road where the solitary nature of the human journey becomes clearly seen. I have never been able to go with a woman, man, or child after his last exhalation. But clearly I have been fascinated with this common transition, this slipping away and its universal heroism. I have danced with death as a woman who wears veils over her eyes so as not to be recognized by her partner, for he may come to where she sleeps and make demands that are hard. The truth may be too brilliant a light, too vast for words or other mental geometries. Perhaps our solitary walk with mortality is indeed only a portion of what is real. Perhaps we are like leaves on the top of a beautiful tree that have no concept of the size of the tree and the manner in which it is attached to the earth. But can we not have some comfort in our ignorance—a vision, a voice? Cannot the small and insignificant Gwynneve be like the saints who saw figures come from another realm and heard their blessing from glowing mouths? I wanted to see Brigit for myself, the mother saint, the protector who came herself to tend her flame, passing from the ephemeral realm into our midst, never blemished, never aged, never muted and diminished as Giannon was.

I am neither ignorant nor rebellious concerning the rule that forbids any human to spy upon Brigit on her night. But I also believe in the unlimited depth of her compassion. It is something I want to feel directly. To know that the thing to which we pray is not emptiness—is that not what our child's soul begs for? I do not want to be a martyr. I want to be Gwynneve with a deeper faith. Then I will go from here. Then I will do penance, not by punishment but by living more freely and more simply.

The night of Brigit's visitation was free of wind and had only a little dampness, which came from the ground in a low and gentle fog. I could see around me clearly by the light of the moon and stars, which were not muted by cloud. I wrapped cloth around my ankles so the chains would not make harsh noise. Still I had to go slowly and with little motions. The darkness and silence in Sister Aillenn's *clochan* seemed watchful and awake. I looked behind me many times and saw no one follow. The chapel was empty, and the flame moved and writhed as though it wished to leave its dish and greet me. Long it took to push the door open and then to close it, for it is a heavy door and full of moans. I turned and studied the chapel, the altar where the flame burns, the hall of benches where nuns' places are separated from monks' by rugs hung on ropes. And I thought, What need will we have of such a separation when all the monks have castrated themselves and all the nuns despise their own bodies?

The flame went low, a sad thing throwing grasping shadows on the stone walls. I thought to replenish the oil myself but prayed to Saint Brigit instead, saying, "You must come. You must let me see you." I sat on the first bench, my ankles sore and tired of the chains. I kneeled and prayed, using the words of the psalm that begins, "The Lord is my shepherd." And I waited. A pebble fell on the floor. A sound like wings came from a dark corner behind me. I will confess that I was afraid, for it occurred to me again that the spirit of a saint or warrior may be a thing made of elements a human cannot survive. The very sight of it may cause the eyes to melt or the flesh to peel from the bones. Perhaps my fear swept the air of any spirit wanting to appear, for then there was silence, and much time went by.

Still on my knees, I thought of my circumstance. I felt the sharp presence of the chains around my ankles and what they meant. This was no game. The man who had put them there had taken a blade to his own body. There was a desperation in him that infected the place. He seemed to want to carve away all solid forms to get to the spirit, like the Roman philosophers who cut up the body to find the gland or organ that is the soul. These Romans were corrupt, and it is no mystery that the people of that empire ran to Christ as their savior. They had been beset for years with worship of mortals as the result of emperors declaring themselves and their concubines to be gods. Christ liberated them. He purified and simplified the divine. He replaced Caligula's whims and Hadrian's obsessions with the simple belief that there is the one God who knows the suffering of every man. Still there lingered the philosophies of those who preferred to attend to theories and ideals rather than suffering.

Plato and others who declare the existence of ideals are like lunatics who remember things that never happened or existed. They have created their own delusions, perhaps for entertainment, or to distract themselves from the knowledge that in order to act upon what is solid, they must develop compassion and courage rather than philosophies. The philosophers who now control the Christian cult and condemn Pelagians as heretics love the ideal as a measure by which to judge those who do not agree with their authority. Whoever reads this, do not be told what to do to receive grace. You know in your heart, unless your mind is sick. And if your mind is sick, then make a country where all the people have sick minds and kill each other over philosophies and hallucinations.

I long for the times when a man's head was severed because another man wanted what he had. Here is a direct motive. I had thought that the love of Christ would make us kinder and less likely to smash skulls. But now I see that we will be asked to smash skulls for Christ. The bishops who love power will surely love a motive so easily manipulated to suit their needs. I have read many powerful men's contradictory ideals and assertions of what Christ meant for us to do and think. If the abbot wants me dead because I am capable of ruining his influence with my knowledge and my ability to speak and write it, then he can use his version of Christ to kill me. He can summon an ideal and show my sin against it. All he needs is his status and the fears and ignorance of others. There is plenty of all three.

After hours of such meditation and agitation in the chapel, I stood, unsteady because I had forgotten that my ankles were bound. Then I knew that I was not alone. I listened without breathing, and I heard breathing that was not my own, which came from behind the rug that separated me from the monk's side. There was someone there, on the other side. The flame sputtered and I crossed myself. Impeded by the chains around my ankles, I walked forward, staring hard at the flame, until I was beside the altar, and I turned to face the benches on the monk's side. The figure sat in the dark and did not move or speak. I asked, "Are you human?" And it did not answer. I whispered, "Brigit?" And the figure bent forward to put its head upon its knees.

I saw then that he was a monk, and when he looked up at me, I knew that it was Giannon. I asked, "Why are you silent?" I was trembling so that I had to sit beside him. He held my head against his chest, and I could feel the tremors of his weeping. After these many years, I said first to Giannon, who was my soul's twin whom I had thought never to meet again in this realm, "I have learned to read and write in Latin. I have transcribed parchment from all over the world, the words of men whose bodies are dust. I have learned what emperors and philosophers and scholars have concluded and what they believe and how they mean to order this world." I was his student, reporting to him as though I had done what was assigned only yesterday, and now I could be done and go on to another task. I wanted to be done. I have seen enough at this place. The flame grew small, and we both looked at it, fearing that even our breath would extinguish it.

I asked, "To what place can we escape?" He still did not speak. I said, "I have written about my life. I have written about the times before and after we lived together. You must read it, for now I think that I was writing it for you." He leaned back, his beard trembling, and closed his eyes but still held on to my hand. I whispered, "What happened to silence you? What has happened all these years? Look how old I am, how my hair is turning gray and my flesh is drying. What has happened to us all these years? Are you still a druid? Are we still druids, Giannon, bards and poets who are free to go from one *túath* to another without enemies? Who are our enemies now, Giannon? And why do we threaten them?" His silence made my words seem as worthless as water pouring over the rim of a cup already full.

Brigit's flame grew dimmer. I whispered, "I came here to see her, to touch the divine and know it existed." And then the flame went out and we were in darkness. I stood up, and we were black forms in the empty chapel. I stared at the place where the flame had been. When I spoke at last, I said, "Let us leave this place, this region. Let us go and never return." Giannon looked up at me then, and I saw the empty, tongueless cavern surrounded by trembling lips and unkempt whiskers. I held his hands tightly and he grasped hard, a weary, broken man who may have been witless. He did not move away, and I remembered when we were so young and he did not embrace long. He kissed my hands, weeping with a noise in his throat that was not human. And I felt a cool peace fall through me like water. I had no words for it. At that time the flame came back, bursting up with a round and hollow sound like a drum being beat. And its light was wild. It was a pagan flame. And in its light I could see the face of Giannon. He was an old man, far older than I. His eyes were shrunken into his head and filled with the milk of old age. His face was a map of years and valleys and streams. He trembled, his head moving in small and constant circles. He was, after all, a mortal man, and I knew that not he nor anyone would rescue me.

I then told my old and weary friend that there were parchments in my *clochan*. I revealed the hiding place among bundles of cloth that no Christian man would touch, for it was used to catch the blood that comes out, infrequently now, from my womb. And so I asked that Giannon take these parchments when I am gone from here if he stays behind. I asked that he read them, for I want some soul in this world to think on what I have seen. I said to Giannon that now that I had finished my training I was allowed three opinions, according to the rules I learned from him many years ago. So I told him then my three opinions, having gained the privilege to give them. He sighed and I spoke, saying, "First, *bairgen* is best when eaten with cream. Second, morning air is more finely perfumed than evening air." I waited, and then an opinion came to me in a woman's voice that I did not recognize as my own. But I believed the words and spoke them: "Third, receiving kindness is the only comfort for suffering. Giving kindness is the only method of forgetting suffering. The creed is of no concern, and the act may be so simple as to seem insignificant, such as the kindness of the sun drying my leggings, or of a hand offering cheese, or of a voice saying, 'I will stay with you.' "

A few breaths after I had spoken, the rug that separated one side of the chapel from the other was torn aside, and we saw there Sister Luirrenn with round and fierce eyes and spittle coming from her toothless mouth. I knew at that moment that everything had changed, that everything in this land and the world had changed. Sister Luirrenn did not seem wise to me anymore. Giannon stood unsteadily, unable to act with any force as Luirrenn and a monk with thick arms led me to my cell, where they drove a stake into the ground for the purpose of attaching my chains to something immovable. Then the abbot fetched the smith from the settlement below, who ran to my *clochan* with his glowing iron. While he did his work, the smith asked to be forgiven, for I had been to his home one or two times to give his family bread after his pigs drowned and to hold his child when it died of a fever. Now I only move in the circle allowed by my tether. I was a tamed wolf; now I have gone feral, not to be trusted. I say, Why not put me back into the wild? I am dangerous only when I am urged to be what I am not.

I have asked about Giannon, still calling him the monk who does not speak. Sister Aillenn spies on him, for she has grown calmer and does not scream at night. She is cunning and has found that her reputation as transcendent saint or deranged specter allows her to go about freely. She has found that Giannon, too, is shackled but allowed to work in the garden, for he is considered harmless, an ineffective old man who is mute. The abbot has come tonight and promises to dig in my cell to discover the bones of children I have buried in the floor after my satyr's feasts. He asked to examine my feces. I remain, like Giannon, silent, word-less in his presence. There is no other recourse but to let him play out his mad attempt and to believe that the sisters, even Aillenn and Luirrenn, will not let harm come to me as a result of false and obscene accusations. Then will Giannon and I go away together, carrying my scrolls, for now I know that my life is ordinary and that it will continue so that I will be an old woman and attend to Giannon when he dies. I will hold his hand and tell him stories about the heroes, Mebd and Cuchulain and Jesus Christ and Brigit.

I see from my doorway that Sister Aillenn has enticed the wild mare to touch its nose to her hand. She stands outside with her hair free and strokes the beast's neck. The stallion is at a distance below them on the hill, and I can just see his head, which he tosses in agitation to see the risk the mare is taking. I think he will find that the seduction is not from human to horse, but from horse to human, and that soon Sister Aillenn will be one of them. Oh, I am glad that there are small freedoms in the world, even if they exist only in the imagination. I am glad that I have stored in my mind certain moments and that I have let myself feel the tickle of an ant on my skin and smelled the perfume of a great storm in the mountains. Praise God for these things. May people protect them and be grateful for them.

Let all who read this know that I am no witch. Let all who read this beware of Christians and druids who claim to put words to that which cannot be named. Use words to please, to instruct, to soothe. Then stop speaking.

EPILOGUE

I HAVE NEWS that should be known.

In the Order of Saint Brigit during the second year of the authority of the abbot named Adrianus, Gwynneve born in Tarbfhlaith was taken from her *clochan* with her ankles shackled. It should be known that she was moved by procession through the small settlement that surrounds the abbey, where people were instructed to throw stones upon her as she walked. Her beauty was great, though she no longer had youth. Her deportment was proud. Those who met her eyes stood still and let their stones drop to the ground beside their own feet. The day was full of light. Though there were many clouds, they were held away from the sun. It should be known that there was fear in Gwynneve's face, which she did not try to disguise, but which did not make her stumble. Thus it happened.

There is more to this news.

A monk named Haldrynn walked behind her and beat upon a drum while announcing that she had caused unnatural deaths and consumed infants. It should be known that one woman among the laypeople ran along with the small procession, pounding her own chest and pulling her own hair. This woman claimed that the nun Gwynneve was innocent, and that she herself had exhumed her own infant in order to give it a sacred burial with pagan methods. She said that it had been her sin to love the newborn greatly and to have looked too deeply into its eyes and should not have attached herself to its frail spirit. The abbot and his cohorts told the woman to silence herself or have her other children taken and buried alive. Thus it happened. It should be known that also in the procession was Sister Aillenn, who leads the nuns since she has been given the position of mother in place of Sister Luirrenn, who has taken ill and requests that her duties be given over, though it should be known that she protested the abbot's choice of successor. Thus it happened.

There is more to this news.

The nun Gwynneve was made to sit upon the edge of the old well that is two Roman miles north of the abbey and just within the woods of Firfhlaith. The sun was above the top of the rowan tree that bows over the well. It should be known that the nun Gwynneve was then pushed backward into the depths of the well by the abbot and his attendant, Haldrynn. No cries came from within the pit, which is said to be as deep as ten men are tall. The woman who had run beside Gwynneve called down to ask if she were suffering, but there was no answer. Thus it happened, and I wept to see it.

Gwynneve of Tarbfhlaith, scribe of the Order of Saint Brigit, lived over forty years in this incarnation. I, Giannon the Mute, have taken her place as scribe at this place, protector of codices and parchment. Her life is presented in her own words on codices that will hereafter be sealed and protected. She has not included in her own words what reputation others have given her, some of it false and much of it true. It has been said that Gwynneve transformed herself as a druid into a wolf and moved about in wilderness and *túath*s as such a beast, bringing both blessing and disaster. These tales relate also her battles with spirit entities, including the altercation with a Formorian incarnated as a bear who sat upon her and would have killed her had she not conjured a spell against it. Thus it is said to have happened.

It should be known that she has herself been inaccurate by excluding the acts that gave her the reputation as a saint, a reputation refuted forcefully by the priests and abbots who pronounce who is saint and who is sinner. Gwynneve disliked hunger and fed those who suffered it. For some time when she was a goatherd, she supplied several *túath*s with milk and cheese when they had been stripped of their goods by rivals. Her greatest fame was as one who attends the deathbed. Her strength was in accompanying a woman, a child, or a man to his final breath. Gwynneve did not turn away from the stench or writhing of death. She was known to say, "I will stay with you." Thus it happened.

There is more to this news.

In her own death, Gwynneve was not false. She said once as she walked to the well, "I am afraid," and then, as she sat on the stones around the well, she addressed the abbot gently, saying, "I wish I could live more." Finally, she said to those who stood around, unable to cast their eyes on her face, that she wanted to be given poison in case she did not die from the fall into the well, and in case there was not water enough to drown her at the distant bottom. The woman who had run beside her said that she would fetch hemlock and throw it down to her if she did not die quickly and suffered wounds and starvation. It should be known that this same woman and others have been seen throwing sprigs of white flowered hemlock into that well and calling down to what lies in its dark and narrow distance. It should be known that all who go to this well add their tears to its waters. It should be known that all who call out Gwynneve's name beg for forgiveness and for help in understanding and overcoming suffering. The answer is always silence.

GLOSSARY

Aes dána · Druids and their companions.

Aimsirtogu · The age of choice: seven for a boy, fourteen for a girl.

Aisling · Mystical vision or dream.

Anamchara · Confessor or authority on cleansing the soul.

Bàdhum · Place where cows are kept.

Baile Shuibhe · Frenzy of Sweeny, who went in search of peace of mind by developing an animal familiarity with nature.

Bairgen · Cake speckled with currants.

Ballcin · Cup or vessel made of wood.

Ban-druí · Female druid.

Bas-chrann · Small wooden log used as a knocker.

Bean sidhe · Woman of the fairies.

Birer · Watercress.

Ceallurach · Cemetery for unbaptized children or suicides.

Cele dé · Servant of a god; nun.

Cíorbolg · Comb bag for women.

Clochan · Beehive-shaped cell made of stone.

Copog phadraig · Common plantain, used to return strength after blood loss.

Corpan fedilfas · Denial of food to the body for spiritual discipline.

Crem · Wild garlic.

Cumal · Unit of bargaining equaling three milk cows or a certain amount of land.

Dabhach · Two-handled tub.

Dal · Land where a tribe exists.

Editorulgatu · Common Latin version of the Bible, based on a translation by Saint Jerome.

Fé · Stick used to measure a person's grave.

Fidchell · A game like chess.

Finna · Royal bodyguard.

Fled co-lige · Feast of the deathbed.

Fortúatha · Of the alien people.

Fraechoga · Woodberries.

Geìlt · One who goes mad and flees from battle.

Gonomil, organmil, morbumil · A chant to kill worms.

Im noin · The one meal served at monasteries, in the afternoon.

Nenadmín · Crabapple cider.

Oblaire · Leader or elder of a troupe of entertainers.

Ogham · Stone on which words and marks were carved, sometimes to mark a grave or place of significance.

Ollam · The highest form of druidic bard.

Sciathlúireach · Protective prayers from one of the books of Saint Patrick.

Screpull · Silver coin.

Tanag · Hard cheese.

Tánaise · Next in line to be chieftain or kin.

Teách Duinn · An island southwest of Ireland where the dead are said to gather.

Túath · Tribe made up of one or more kinship groups or clans.